MW00652758

THE HEIR

GEORGIA LE CARRE

THE HEIR

I thought he was a player.
How could I have possibly known what he really was?

Georgia Le Carre

Many thanks to:

Editors: Caryl Milton, Elizabeth Burns
Contributors: IS Creations
Cover Designer: ReddHott Covers
Proofreader: Nicola Rhead
Last minute proofing : Brittany Urbaniak & Tracy Gray

The Heir

Copyright © 2017 by Georgia Le Carre

The right of Georgia Le Carre to be identified as the Author of the Work has been asserted by her in accordance with the copyright, designs and patent act 1988.

All rights reserved. No part of this publication may be reproduced, stored in a retrieval system, or transmitted, in any form or by any means without the prior written permission of the publisher, nor be otherwise circulated in any form of binding or cover other than that which it is published and without a similar condition being imposed on the subsequent purchaser.

All characters in this publication are fictitious, any resemblance to real persons, living or dead, is purely coincidental.

You can discover more information about Georgia Le Carre and future releases here.

978-1-910575-65-9

CHAPTER 1

Rosa

https://www.youtube.com/watch?v=BT4GIljqr-A
(Can't take my eyes off you)

"*C iao bella.*"

The voice is dripping honey with a hint of something dark and delicious, but that trite phrase, though. Someone please stop me from picking up my fork and stabbing it into his crotch. I let my eyes wander away from the white tablecloth. Hang on! That is one full crotch. Looks like there is something very large tucked away beneath those fine black trousers. Hmmm …

A little higher. All right. The man works out. If my washing machine packs up I could wash my clothes on his abs.

I let my eyes travel even higher. Did someone say pecs and abs? Drool, drool.

Whoa. Open shirt.

Two buttons undone: check.

Chest hair: check.

Gold chain: check.

St Tropez tan: check.

Black hair curling over the collar: Check.

What a shame. Mediterranean playboy, obviously. Still, I'm a sucker for a brown throat.

No, no, no, not a chin dimple as well. A little above the lickable dimple a sensual mouth is slightly twisted into a mocking smile. Yup, life's just not fair.

Eyes. Jesus. H. Christ. Pools of smooth whiskey that you just want to drown in. There's no longer any doubt. He's obviously slept with tons of women.

The mouth opens. "You know, I've never banged a bridesmaid before."

Why does God make such good-looking assholes? "Looks like today's not your lucky day either," I say dryly.

The smug smile becomes wider, the man is oozing confidence and something else. Something that makes me want to bite him. On his butt. He lowers that wonderful body into the chair opposite. "On the contrary, I think today is that day."

"Oh yeah? How do you reckon that? There are three of us. Raven is pregnant, Cindy is taken, and I'm not interested."

He leans back and looks at me curiously. "What makes you think you're not interested?"

"What makes you think I am?" I counter.

"Because I'd make the perfect one-night stand."

I look at the rose petal floating in my glass of champagne. Star will be so irritated to see it. She expressly said she didn't want it. I look into his mesmerizing eyes. "I'm not looking for a one-night stand."

He grins. He has splendid teeth. All white and gleaming. "Ah, but you are a career woman. You have no time for relationships and long-term commitment."

Something in my belly melts. "I'm not sleeping with you."

"Who said anything about sleeping?"

There is very little air in my lungs suddenly. "I'm not fucking you."

"Ten bucks says you do."

"What would I do with ten bucks in this country?" I ask scornfully.

"I'll take you to America and you can spend it there."

"That's not how one-night stands work."

"No, I meant I'll fly you there tonight. We'll have sex in a great hotel, then you can spend your money in the morning."

"If I have sex with you then I won't have the ten bucks to spend, will I?"

"You'll have more than ten bucks." He takes an expensive looking wallet out of his trouser pocket and fishes out five crisp hundred-dollar bills and lays them on the table."

WTF! My eyes widen with shock. I look at the money and his large, bronzed hand, a gold watch peeping from a snowy white sleeve, slowly sliding away on the white tablecloth. How dare he? Calmly, I take my gaze back to his face. "First of all, five hundred dollars? How cheap are you? And second, do I look like a prostitute to you?"

"First of all: Baby, come with me and I'll make this ten, twenty, fifty, or even a hundred thousand? Name your price." He shrugs. "Secondly: you don't pay a woman to have sex with her, you pay her to leave after sex, and we both know you'll probably sneak out in the morning before I wake up."

I cross my arms and his eyes drop to my breasts. "Excuse me. My face is up here, buster."

"I know exactly where your face is, *bella*. I was looking at your boobs."

I glare at him. "It's a bit sad when you have to flash Daddy's money around just to get laid."

"Very sad," he agrees with a grin, completely unaffected by my insult.

"Who are you?" I demand. He's obviously from the groom's side.

"I'm Dante D'Angelo, and you are Rosa."

My lips part. In spite of myself I'm flattered that he was interested enough to find out my name. "How do you know that?"

"I asked the bride."

I nod. "So how do you know the groom?"

"We're friends." For the first time, something in his eyes change. My mind notes the shift. He's not *all* player, there's something more beneath the glittering facade.

He leans forward slightly, his whiskey eyes swirling with desire. "Do you want to know what the bride told me?"

I frown. What on earth could Star have told him about me. "What?"

"She said, you would be perfect for me."

My eyes dart to the dance floor. She is slow-dancing, her cheek laying on her new husband's chest. I don't know what I expected, but never that. She's usually so rational and down to earth. The stress of the wedding must have affected her so much she's told a pampered, Italian playboy I'm perfect for him. Either that or he's lying.

"Well, I'm not going to bed with you." My voice is absolutely firm. I'll never go to bed with a shallow beast like him. Never. Not in a million years. He can take his gorgeous teeth, and his splendid shoulders, and his laughing, teasing eyes, and his … his … full crotch, and shove it all up his ass.

CHAPTER 2

Rosa
One Month Later

"*Y*ou're what?" Star screams in my ear.

I hold the phone away. "I'm pregnant," I repeat.

"How?"

"The usual way, I guess?"

"Who?" Poor thing is so shocked she's shooting one word questions at me.

"You'll never believe me if I told you."

"Who?" she demands aggressively.

"Dante D'Angelo."

"What?" she explodes.

"Do you want me to repeat his name or are you just saying that for effect?"

"But you used a condom."

"Yeah, we did. I was thinking of suing the makers when I happened to read the packaging. Did you know that there is a one percent chance of getting pregnant even when you use a condom? It says so right here on the packaging."

"No."

"Those are terrible odds. God, if I had known earlier I would have made him wear two layers, but that would only reduce the odds to one in two hundred. We need a new invention. Either that or we'll all have to stop having all this sex and—"

"Rosa, are you okay?"

"What do you think? I'm calling you from my bathroom floor."

"Did you fall? Are you all right? Do you want me to come around?"

"No. Yes. No. I … err … am sitting propped up against the bath. I don't think it has properly registered yet. I'm saving my total meltdown for later."

She takes a deep breath. "Do you need an audience for that? I'm in Mayfair so I can pop around."

"It won't be pretty," I warn. I can already feel my body starting to shake. Mother of God, I'm pregnant.

"How many times did you do the test?"

"Five."

"Right. You're pregnant."

"You're hurting my ear, Star."

"Sorry."

"It's not your fault. It's that smooth-talking bastard's fault. He got me into this. I've been having sex since I was seventeen, and nothing like this has ever happened. One night with that, that, pampered Casanova and I'm pregnant. Of all the damn men I could have got up the duff with I had to go do it with that shallow womanizer."

"Are you going to keep it?" Her voice is neutral, but I can hear the anxiety in it. Star loves kids. She coos at random babies in the street, and she's been buying and hoarding baby clothes for years now.

I have a sudden image of Dante's gleaming, taut body rippling as he thrust into me. I hate him, obviously, but for God's sake, he removed my panties with his yummy teeth … and he was really, really, reeeeeally good at what he did. I couldn't walk properly for days afterwards.

"I don't know yet," I say, but even as I am saying it I have an image of a barefoot little urchin with black hair and whiskey eyes running wild in a field. Which is stupid, because I live in one of the most concrete parts of London. I'll have to drive at least an hour to find a field. Even if I did that I would never trust my child to run barefoot, because of rusty nails, dog poop, and whatever else would be in open fields.

"Bastard," I curse soundly, as if it's all Dante's fault and I didn't beg for him to do it harder and faster.

"You mean you might keep it?"

"Maybe," I say slowly.

"Oh, Rosa," she breathes excitedly. "You should. It'll be such fun. I could take care of it while you are at work or when you go out at night. If it gets too much, or you need a break you could drop it off at our place and—"

"Star," I interrupt, "do you mind? You're making a baby sound like a suitcase."

"Well, in a way it is."

"Yeah, a suitcase full of vomit and poo."

"They're gorgeous," she defends.

"They scream all night."

"No, they don't."

"Yes, they do. I have first-hand experience. The brat next door never stops screaming all night."

"He has colic."

"What if my baby has it?" Jesus, I can't believe I said that. I'm thinking of the baby as a little person. My little person. All for me. "Oh, my God, Star. I think I'm going to keep the baby."

"You'll have to tell the father then," she gushes.

I thought I'd never see him again when I slipped out of his hotel room that morning while he was still asleep. Maybe, I haven't thought this decision out properly. I'm never, not in a million years, seeing that guy again.

Never.

And I mean never.

CHAPTER 3

Rosa

I stand in the lobby of one of Rome's finest hotels and smooth down my skirt. I've heard of people living in the penthouses of hotels during the 1940s and 50s, but honestly, whoever does that anymore?

Of course, a real life Italian playboy with more money than sense. Still, it's a turn up for the books. Who'd ever have imagined I'd meet one of those let alone sleep with him? Then carry his baby inside my body.

A liveried porter meets my gaze. I nod confidently at him and start walking towards the golden reception. I'm not kidding. It actually looks like it's carved out of a massive block of gold. A dark-haired beauty greets me politely.

"I'm here to see Mr. D'Angelo. I believe he resides here."

The reaction is impressively quick. Her smile freezes in its upward track. "Of course you are," she says in a bored voice. "Is he … expecting you?"

I feel my hackles rising. What does she think? I'm one of those women who just turn up unannounced to throw themselves at the playboy of the century? I take a deep breath. I stop my fingers from tapping the polished counter. It's not her fault. This probably happens a lot. It's totally understandable. Must be extremely annoying. I look around me. "Do you have a café or a bar here?"

"We have both."

"Where is the café?"

Holding the bored, superior expression, she points down a corridor. "Turn left at the end of it."

I smile. "Good. Could you kindly tell him that I will be waiting in the café?"

"Rosa?"

Damn. The deep smooth voice makes a shiver run down my spine. I don't turn around, but I see him in the expression on the face of the beauty in front of me. Hell, if anyone had told me someone could change like that I wouldn't have believed it. Like a two-bar heater she begins to radiate and glow from the inside. I want to stay and watch, but I have bigger problems to face.

Slowly, I turn around, the smile I had practiced in the mirror plastered on my face. Oh, my God, no wonder I slept with him. I was tipsy that time, but in the light of the day, I feel my heart begin to pound. Only gay guys are ever this good looking. Look at that plump bottom lip. I remember sucking it into my mouth. Oh shit. This is not exactly going to plan.

I clear my throat. "Dante."

He smiles slowly, his eyes roaming my face. *"Ciao bella."*

I close my eyes for a second. Yes, I remember now. He is not daddy material. I've just got to break the bad news to him and catch my plane, which leaves in less than three hours.

I open my eyes. "Can I talk to you for a bit?"

"Of course. We can … talk upstairs. It'll be more comfortable."

"No," I blurt out. "We'll talk in the café. I'd like a cup of coffee." I jerk my chin towards the café.

His eyes widen with surprise. Fucking bastard! He actually thought I flew all the way over here to have sex with him! God, the arrogance of some people.

"I have coffee upstairs," he drawls.

"I'm sure you do, but the café is nearer. Besides, I don't have a lot of time. My flight is in less than three hours." Put that in your pipe and smoke it, you ripped, sexy Casanova, you.

Now his eyebrows take an upward flight. "But *bella*, I have a bed upstairs."

I need to spill some hot coffee on him. I open my mouth to say something cutting, so it might have been a good thing that we are interrupted by another sultry beauty. She is flowing out of a black mini dress. She also has the most perfect face I've ever seen. I should get her number. One of the photographers I know is looking for just that type of sulky beauty for a shoot in Morocco.

"Dante," she pouts. She has the kind of voice that grates on my nerves. Way worse than a fingernail on a blackboard.

He turns to look at her. I watch with interest as her face too flickers and starts shining like a light bulb.

He frowns at her. "What are you doing here?"

"I should be asking what are you doing with that prostitute?" she asks in Italian, glaring at me. Luckily, or unluckily for me I learned both French and Italian when I decided to go into fashion. Though I butcher the language when I try to speak it, I can understand it.

"Don't worry," I say, breaking into the loving couple's little domestic interaction. "I won't keep him long. I have a flight to catch in …," I look at my watch, "exactly two hours and forty-nine minutes."

Some of the hostility leaves her eyes. "Oh." She winds herself around him and looks adoringly up at him. "Shall I wait for you to finish?"

Dante throws a mocking look my way, before he turns to her and says, "Go upstairs, take your clothes off, and sit on my bed with your legs wide open." He looks again at me and there is a challenging glint in his eyes, but I manage to keep my face totally impassive.

I know he only did that to rile me, but my stomach clenches hard. I am suddenly so jealous and furious I feel like punching him in the face.

"I'll be waiting for you at the café," I say as calmly as I can, and begin walking in the direction of the corridor.

He falls into step next to me. "Do you know you look even more beautiful today than you did the last time I saw you? You are … glowing."

I don't look at him. "Will you give it a rest?"

"I think you should report it to the police."

My heels click loudly on the granite floor as I walk briskly towards the café. "Report what?"

"Someone stole your smile."

If I wasn't so angry I might have smiled, but I was alternating between jealousy at the thought of the beauty going to his suite to wait for him, and boiling fury at his arrogance. "Very funny. Ha, ha."

"Why are you so angry, *bella*?"

"Will you quit calling me that?"

"Why not? You are beautiful."

13

We have reached the café so I huff audibly and walk into it. There is only one table taken up by an elderly couple. Gentility oozes out of their pores. They glance discreetly at us as we enter. Well, they are about to hear an earful. "I didn't come here to be flattered, or to sleep with you so you can stop laying it on so thick."

"Why did you come?"

I head toward the table at the very back of the opulent room. As my butt hits the plush armchair, a waiter in a dark suit materializes at our side. He has cunning dark eyes. He smiles up at Dante with an expression that hovers between obsequiousness and greed. I guess Dante must be a great tipper.

"Your usual, padrone?" he asks in Italian.

Dante nods.

Then the waiter turns toward me. "*Signorina*," he greets with a little foxy nod.

I order an espresso.

"Nothing to eat?" Dante asks, one dark eyebrow raised.

I shake my head.

"I can recommend the club sandwich," the waiter adds.

"Thank you, but no," I say.

He nods politely and makes himself scarce.

I try not to watch as Dante lowers his magnificent body into the armchair opposite me.

He catches my eye and gives one of those nonchalant shrugs that only people from the Mediterranean can get away with. "So ... to what do I owe the pleasure of this meeting?"

I clear my throat. "I have some news for you, although it actually does not need to affect you at all ...if you don't want it to."

He smiles mockingly. "And what would that be?"

I take a deep breath. "I'm pregnant."

He stills, but the words that come out of his mouth don't match the stillness. "Congratulations, *bella*."

This is not at all how I envisioned this exchange. It is all going wrong. I shift uncomfortably. "It's yours."

For just a fraction of a heartbeat something flashes in his eyes. He is not Dante D'Angelo the playboy. He is a sophisticated entity that I have underestimated. During that infinitesimally small fraction of time I feel the ground beneath me shift. Everything is not as it seems. Then the mask drops back into place, and he sits forward, his eyes narrowed. "You are pregnant with *my* child?"

I nod.

"How do you know it is mine?" he asks softly.

"Because I haven't been with anyone else for more than a year."

He stares at me, surprised. It's insulting, but how can I blame him for feeling surprised. Two hours after meeting him I was in his hotel room with my legs around his neck.

He leans back and regards me without any expression at all. I don't say a word, but I must confess this is not at all the reaction I thought I would get.

He massages his bottom lip with his thumb.

It triggers a memory. Without thinking, my tongue comes out to lick my own lips.

The waiter comes back still smiling smarmily. He settles all the items onto a tray on the table as if he is performing a magic trick. I smile my thanks, but Dante completely ignores him. I watch Dante reach for the sugar tongs before looking up at me. He raises his eyebrows.

I shake my head and he drops two cubes into his own expresso. His expression is so veiled. I can't make out anything of what is going on in his head. He takes the little spoon from the saucer. God, those brown hands. I remember them inside me. I take a sudden sharp breath, and his eyes rise up and meet mine. He stares at me while he swirls the sugar into his coffee. I want to look away, but I can't. He lifts his cup to his lips and downs his espresso with a slight tip of his head. He puts the cup down.

"I presume that you are planning on keeping our child if you are telling me about it."

My heart stops beating. Holy hell, did I just hear him say our child? "Yes, I am planning on keeping it, but I don't expect any support, or help from you. You are not required to do anything."

"Hmmm." He leans back, his knees wide open, and looks at me. It is a totally confident, dominating Alpha pose.

I shift nervously in my seat. "I just wanted you to know, because it's right that you should. If you don't want me to tell him about you when he is old enough now is the time to speak."

His eyes are like lasers. "What if I want to be in my child's life?"

My eyebrows rise. "Of course, you're welcome to visit him anytime you want. I have no problem with that. In fact, I think it would be a good thing for the kid."

"What if I want to have him live with me?"

I blink. "What?"

"What if I want to have him live with me?"

"I heard you, I just didn't understand what you meant."

"I want you and the baby to live with me."

This time my mouth drops open. "What?"

16

"I want you and—"

"Don't do that. This is not a joke. I can't live with you. To start with you live in a hotel."

"I could live in a house," he says quietly.

"Is this your idea of a serious conversation?"

"Why not? We could live together in this beautiful city. Share the burden of parenting."

I snort. "Oh yeah? So what you are suggesting is we live together, but live separate lives. You'd be free to bring all your women home and I'd have to listen to them screaming away in your bedroom."

A small smile tips the side of his lips. "You could be the one screaming in my bedroom."

"That's never going to happen."

"Have you forgotten, *Cara,* how much you screamed when I was inside you?"

My whole face burns with embarrassment. "You are no gentleman."

"There you go. We already understand each other perfectly."

"You're mad. Such an arrangement would *never* work. I'd end up stabbing you in the eye while you are sleeping."

He frowns. "A child needs both its parents, Rosa."

"Look, this is not a conversation I came to have with you. I'm not going to live with you. I have my life in England, and my career that I have worked so hard to build. So please forget any crazy idea that I'm going to come here to Rome to play house with you. We are not in love. I'm not even sure I like you. This was an accident and while it's not the greatest news in the world, it doesn't have to be the worst. We can both be mature about this."

His expression doesn't change and I take a deep breath and carry on.

"I'll contact you after the baby is born, and if you still want to be in his or her life we'll work something out. I'm not an unreasonable person. I want my child to have access to its father, especially if he wants it too."

My little prepared speech is over so I stand and look down at him. Jesus, is there any angle from which this guy doesn't look good? Thank God, I won't be seeing much of him because he causes my body to go haywire. "Well, I should be going. You have a naked woman waiting upstairs for you and I have a plane to catch. So ... *ciao, Bello.*"

His lips curve upwards, and a completely wicked smile plays on his mouth. "Have a safe flight."

Bastard. I don't hang around.

CHAPTER 4

Dante

I watch her leave. Her back rigid, and the soft curves of her small ass hidden under her manly jacket. And those calves. I remember the feel of them. My gut tightens with the memory. She has great legs. Long and shapely. I still remember opening them. What was between them.

My cock is suddenly achingly hard.

The waiter comes to tell me that a woman has called down from my suite to speak to me.

"Tell her to get dressed and go home." My voice is cold and callous.

His eyebrows flick upwards. He nods politely. "Certainly, Signori Dante."

He walks away and I look at her coffee cup. Untouched. She didn't even pretend to drink it. I steeple my fingers together and think of her furious face. I have known countless women and, in my experience, the women that look strong and tough on the outside are like marshmallows on the inside. The ones you have to watch out for are the ones that appear vulnerable and soft on the outside. They are the ones with the hearts of tempered steel. I know hidden away inside that hard exterior is a heart of gold.

Still, it's a strange and unexpected thing that she should hook me so easily. She is not beautiful in the traditional sense. Her mouth is too wide, her jaw too strong, but there is something about her that I find more beautiful than any woman alive. She makes my blood stir in a way that no other woman has.

That dim morning I was awake. I heard her picking up her clothes from the floor, once accidentally bumping into a chair and cursing quietly. I should have been glad. The next morning is always the tricky part of every hook up and she was taking that unpleasant task away, but some part of me didn't want her to go. I wanted to stop her from leaving. I couldn't understand it. When she was gone I stood at the window and watched her leave the hotel. She looked so small, her red hair like a flame in the wind.

That morning I left England. The country seemed grey and wet and utterly without charm. I took a flight to Monaco. I knew women there. Lots of eager, beautiful women who knew how the game was played. I gambled, I partied, and I tried to forget her, but she was always there. In a dream, in the flash of another woman's skirt.

I never forgot her laugh. Sexy and deep-throated.

I told myself I had a lifestyle and she wouldn't fit in, but I couldn't stop missing the feel of her skin, the way she called out my name when I was deep inside her. My mother told me when I was twenty-three. You can run as far as you want, my son, but you can never run away from your fate. I never believed it, but fate had come to look for me. How mother will laugh when I tell her.

I let her run once. I'm not doing it again. This time everything will be different. She won't stand a chance. I want her and I want my child.

And I know just how to get them too.

CHAPTER 5

Rosa

I cross the grand lobby. My heart is pounding. I'm not sure what I feel. I think I am angry, but I can't be sure. My body feels stiff and tight. It's a feeling I've never had before. I walk out of the hotel and into the street. Shocking. That man's behavior is shocking. He treated the whole thing as if it was a joke. Incredible. Just incredible.

A car screeches to a halt next to me.

Jesus, I just walked in front of a cab. I turn my head and see a man in a taxi. He is red-faced with anger. He swears at me in Italian. I step back and automatically apologize. The man makes a rude gesture with his hand. Yeah, fuck off.

A man's voice comes from my right and I turn towards it.

"Are you all right?" he asks in Italian. He has kind eyes.

I nod and thank him. After he walks away, I manage to flag down a Milano 22 cab. My hands shake as I open the door.

"Fiumicino," I tell him, and with a nod he steps on the gas. I stare blankly out of the windows as he swears and curses at the other drivers on the road. After I have paid him I go into the airport and check in. I am in no mood to shop so I wander through the terminal aimlessly. When my flight is called, I get into the plane and find my seat. Obediently, I fasten my seatbelt when the sign comes on. I stare out of the window as the plane takes off. Goodbye, Rome. The air hostess comes around with the drinks trolley, and I ask for an apple juice. The woman sitting next to me reads a book while I lean back and close my eyes.

When the plane touches down, I walk down those anony-mous corridors with all the other passengers. I pass through Immigration and, since I have no luggage, walk through the green Nothing to Declare door and out through the swing doors.

There are people waiting at the barriers for their loved ones. I planned to take a taxi back, but to my surprise, I see Star. Her large bodyguard is standing behind her. As usual, he looks like he has a poker up his ass. Surrounded by men in dark suits carrying placards with the names of the passen-gers, Star looks like a beautiful angel. She catches my eyes and frowns at me worriedly. I smile reassuringly at her and she smiles back.

Unable to wait for me to get to the end of the barrier, she rushes over to me and envelopes me in a huge hug.

"I love you," she says.

I feel the backs of my eyes start to burn. I'm not going to cry. No, I'm not. I have no reason to cry. My life is good. I have everything the way I want it. I blink hard and the sensation goes away.

She takes my hands. Hers are warm and soft. Her beautiful eyes search my face anxiously. "Your hands are cold. Are you cold?"

I shake my head. I'm not lying. I'm not cold at all.

"Come," she says, and leads me away. Outside, the sky is grey, and it is less warm than it was in Rome. Her blacked-out Mercedes is waiting. We pile into it and the car pulls away.

I turn to look at her. "Thank you for coming to pick me up. I didn't expect you to."

She shrugs. "I wanted to make sure you were all right. Are you?"

I nod and smile broadly so that she can stop worrying about me.

"What happened?"

I frown. How strange. The meeting with Dante feels as if it happened a long time ago. "He wanted me to move to Rome and for us to bring up the baby together."

Her eyes become saucers. "What?"

"Yes, that was his grand plan."

"Are you going to?"

I shake my head. "Of course not. He's no good, Star."

"People can change."

"While he was talking with me, he had a naked woman waiting for him in his suite upstairs."

Her hands drop into her lap. "Oh."

"Yes, oh."

"I'm sorry."

"Don't be. I'm not. It's not like I love him or anything. There were no promises made. It was just a one-night stand, pure and simple. He promised me fun and he kept his side of the bargain. I definitely had fun. It is completely my decision to have this baby. I knew I was going to do it on my own and that is fine by me. I just wanted to let him know so that I could move on knowing I had done the right thing. I've done it now and I'm good. All good."

Star threads her fingers through mine. "For what it's worth, I would have done exactly the same thing you have."

"I know, Star. I know you would have."

She beams at me. "It'll be fun, you'll see. This baby will have so much love poured on it, it won't know what to do with it."

I laugh. "It's not a dog. It has to go to school, get a job when it is older, marry, and have its own kids so you're not allowed to spoil it."

"You're not allowed to spoil it. I am," she says smugly.

I squeeze her hand back. Maybe it's going to be all right. I don't need a man just to help me bring up a baby. I've got the best support system I could ever ask for.

Star's phone rings. She looks at the screen. "Oh, it's Cindy." She hits accept and puts her on speaker.

"Is she there yet?" Cindy asks.

"Yup, got her here."

"Is she all right?"

"I think so. Talk to her. You're on speaker."

"Hey, Cin," I say cheerfully.

"Did you switch your phone off? I've been trying to call you for ages," she complains.

"Yeah, it's off. I haven't switched it back on yet."

"What did he say?"

"He wants us to bring up the baby together."

"He did? Oh my God. That's great," she screams into my ear.

"I'm not bringing the baby up with him, Cin."

"Oh. Why not?"

"Because he's a terrible womanizer. Because he lives in Rome. Because I don't like him. And finally, because I just don't want to."

"Right. Okay. Got it."

"Listen, I'll call you back a bit later when I get settled in, okay?"

"Okay. Speak later, babe."

I look at Star and she opens her mouth. "Don't say it, Star. Just don't say it."

She closes her mouth.

"Let's talk about you. What's going on with you?" I ask in a determined voice.

We spend the rest of the journey to my place talking about an author's convention that she has to attend. It is an exciting thing for her, and I put my own thoughts back and concentrate on her. I am so proud of Star. How high she has flown since her first husband caged her.

Star asks if I want her to come in, but I tell her I need to be alone.

"Do you want to join Nikolai and me for dinner?"

"Thanks, but not tonight."

She peers at me with concern. "Do you want me to come over and have dinner with you?"

"No, you go ahead and have a good time with your husband. I'm fine. I'm just tired. I'll probably get a takeaway and go to bed early."

"If you change your mind, call me, all right?"

I stretch my lips and smile broadly. "Okay. Thanks."

She leaves and I go up to my apartment and close the front

door. I take a deep breath. This is my life. These four walls. That whole thing with Dante was just a piece of fantasy. It is time to put it all behind me. Once and for all.

I go into my bedroom, strip naked, and walk to my bathroom. I switch on the shower and stand under it. The water is deliciously warm. I love being in the shower. The sensation of water washing away everything. Sometimes when I get stuck for ideas I stand here and new inspiration comes flowing into my brain. Today my brain feels empty.

Numb.

The sobs come suddenly from somewhere deep inside me. At first I don't even realize I'm crying. It is only when my whole body starts jerking with the strength of the sobs and my face is scrunched so tight that I recognize I am howling. I slide down the glass wall and slump on the floor. Water cascades down my body, bouncing on my head, my nose, my chin, dripping down my throat.

I don't know why I'm crying.

I put it down to hormones. It's hormones. Of course, it is. It's not disappointment. Just hormones. The baby. The changes going on inside my body. Besides, I'm also tired. As if I have taken the world on my shoulders.

I'll get out of the shower and have a nap. A nap will refresh me and put everything back into perspective.

CHAPTER 6

Rosa

I push open the glass door embossed with the bold black letters that spell out the name of the magazine, *Mirabel.* Entering the white and pink space, I nod to the receptionist sitting behind her glossy counter. There is a blue neon sign above her head that flashes out the magazine's creed.

HAVE IT ALL

I dash into the lift just as the doors are closing, but regret it almost instantly. Someone in the lift is wearing a cloying sweet perfume that makes me want to retch. I really hope and pray morning sickness doesn't become a big thing for me. I get off at the second floor and take the stairs.

As I enter my department, Mary Withers waves me over, calling out, "Morning, Rosa." When I get closer, she drops her voice to a whisper. "The old dragon wants to see you in her lair right away. I have orders to tell you to go in before you become involved in anything else."

Willa wants to see me first thing on Monday morning. I try to think what could have gone wrong and come up with nothing. "Hmmm. Do you know what she wants?"

She pulls a sour face. "Damned if I know."

"Okay. Thanks. I'll go see her now," I say and head down the corridor. I really love my job as a fashion writer, and even Willa Smithton, my direct boss and the executive editor of *Mirabel*, cannot make me love it any less.

I pass my office and hurry next door to hers. I knock on the door. Her office is almost a duplicate of mine, except that it's twice as large and has two windows in the back rather than just one.

"Enter," her gravelly voice commands.

I open the door and stand just inside her office. "Mary said you wanted to see me."

She lifts her head from the papers she is reading and smiles. Willa is a woman of indeterminate age—she could be anything between forty-five and eighty. Nobody has dared ask.

"Well, it seems congratulations are in order."

Congratulations? What on earth is she talking about? I allow my lips to stretch into a polite smile. "Er, what for?"

She is still smiling but her eyes are glittering. "It seems you have suddenly become the head honcho at our sister magazine in Rome."

My jaw drops to the floor. "What?" I nearly shout.

"Yes. I received word early this morning. You could be the

editor of *Mirabel* in Rome—that is, if you agree to take the job."

Suddenly, I feel lightheaded. "I have to sit down," I croak.

Willa waves towards one of the chairs in front of her desk.

"Thank you." The word editor swims around in my head as I sink into one of the winged chairs. I stare at her in shock. "Are you sure this is not some mistake or misunderstanding?"

"I don't make mistakes," Willa snaps.

"It's just … Rome! I can't believe it. It's … it's totally unexpected. I mean, editor. How? Why?" I snap my mouth shut. I'm babbling wildly and Willa hates even mild babbling.

Willa's sharp little eyes regard me expressionlessly. "Yes, I did wonder if it was a mistake, but I spoke to the executive director in our head office in Milan."

"But Rome though," I repeat incredulously.

She sighs. "Yes, if you take away the strutting men, the whiny women, and triple parking, I suppose, it is a beautiful city. Lovely fountains." She pauses. "There's no doubt you'll take the position, is there?"

"I'd certainly be a fool not to. Oh, my God, I'll be living in Rome!"

"If you're going to work there, you'd better live there too, don't you think?" she remarks dryly.

"Unless this is some sort of dream?"

"Or a nightmare?"

My eyes widen with surprise.

"Surely, you don't expect me to celebrate. You're my best writer." Her voice is grudging.

"Oh."

She cracks a reluctant smile. "We'll all miss you."

"I'll miss everyone too," I say automatically, even though nothing could be further from the truth. Other than Mary, most of my colleagues are extremely competitive. They would quite cheerfully stick a knife in my back if it means getting ahead on the ladder of success.

"You won't have time. You'll be too busy putting your own stamp on that magazine."

"It's already pretty darned good, I suspect." I shake my head. "Do you know how all this came about? What happened to the previous editor?"

"That information would fall under the realm of pure gossip."

"Why me?

"Apparently, Angelo Ricci's granddaughter is a big fan of yours. She loves your style—the wit and the humor. Reads everything you write."

"She is?" I gasp. Angelo Ricci is the billionaire owner of Mirabel. His granddaughter is a fan of my work!

"At least that's what I've been told. Once the position opened, she persuaded her grandfather that you were the one for the job."

"Which one of his granddaughters?" I ask curiously.

"Gina Ricci."

I shake my head to clear it. I think I'm too stunned to think. Gina Ricci is a beautiful socialite butterfly. I had no idea she even read, let alone my column. "Wow! This is all too much to take in. When am I supposed to start?"

"Next week, from what I understand."

"Next week! But there's so much to do."

"You could always refuse the job," she says slyly.

"Are you kidding? I'd kill for this job."

The button on her phone blinks and she waves her hand. "Well, you better get on with your day. I still need that Ten Sex Tips article from you."

I jump up from my chair. "Thank you, Willa. Thank you. You'll have the article by tonight."

I walk straight over to Mary's desk.

"Will you pinch me, Mary?"

"What?"

"Pinch me," I order with a laugh.

"Why?"

"I want to know if I'm dreaming."

"All right," she says and pinches me hard.

"Ouch," I yelp and look at her with a surprised, wounded expression.

"There you go. You're not dreaming, and I'm just a little bit envious about why I'm having to pinch you after you've been in the dragon's lair."

I grin. "A little?"

"Okay. A lot. Now, what the bleeding fuck happened in there?"

CHAPTER 7

Rosa

*T*he rest of the day passes in a blur. I'm in such an excited state, I hardly know what I'm doing. On the way out I decide to treat myself to a taxi, even though I live only a few blocks away. Once home, I kick off my shoes, shuck off my jacket, and without even bothering to hang it in the downstairs closet, I pick up my phone and head over to my couch. I curl up and FaceTime Star.

"You'll never guess what," I said when she comes on.

"Judging by your expression it must be brilliant news."

"Unbelievably brilliant," I tell her, as I lean my head back against the buttery softness of the old leather. I'm so going to miss this sofa in Rome. "They want me as editor of the Italian arm of the magazine. I'm going to Rome!"

"What? You're kidding!" she screams.

"No, I'm not."

Her reply is to leave the phone on its holder, fly off the sofa, and start doing a crazy dance all around the room. All I catch is her body zipping past.

Grinning at her antics, I shout out, "Stop that and come back here."

She comes back laughing. "I want to know everything."

"When I got to work this morning, Mary told me the dragon wanted to see me right away. Naturally, I thought I was in trouble, but Willa gives me this news."

"It's so incredible. This is what you have dreamed of all your life. Remember when we were kids and you told everybody that one day you were going to be the editor of a magazine in France or Italy."

I chew on my lower lip. "Uh huh. I remember."

"So how long is it for?"

"I don't know all the details. The contract is being couriered over to me tomorrow from Milan. If I accept I'm supposed to leave next week."

Her voice drops an octave. "If I accept? What does that mean?"

"It means I'm crazy excited about the prospect, but something is bugging me."

Her forehead creases. "It's not the baby, is it?"

"No."

She sits cross-legged and leans her chin on her knee. "Then what problem can keep you away from Rome, the most romantic city in the world, well, apart from Venice in spring, of course?"

"That's part of the problem. Maybe the biggest problem of all."

"What on earth are you going on about?"

I push my hair away from my neck. Even thinking about him makes me hot. "In a word, Dante."

She grins. "Dante? Your playboy."

I roll my eyes. "Not my playboy, Star. Definitely not mine."

"Fine, but quite honestly, I don't see what the problem is."

"He lives there with his one thousand and one girlfriends, Star."

"I know that, but he's the father of your child, and you really should start getting to … know him better." Her expression is serious, but her eyes are twinkling.

"Whose side are you on?"

"Yours, obviously."

I sigh. "It would be a totally different matter if I was not up the duff. Now I'm going to be in Rome with the job of my dreams, the man who terrifies me, and I'm going to have a baby. I'm worried about juggling the three things in a foreign land. I won't even have mum at hand to help out."

"Haven't you heard of nannies, Rosa?"

"I can't get my head around the idea of entrusting my newborn baby to a total stranger. Haven't you seen the You Tube video of women abusing the children in their care? Actually, I'm freaking out just thinking about it now."

"I love you, Rosa, but you're crazy. Why are we even having this conversation now? The baby is not here yet. Plus, didn't Dante say he wanted to play a bigger part in bringing up his child?"

"Hand *my* baby over to that Casanova? No way. He's a complete animal." I have a sudden image of the way he growled while he ate me out. Heat spreads through my body. I scowl at the phone as I burn that image away. "He's almost uncivilized. I bet he has pineapple on his pizza."

35

She giggles. "Oh, don't."

"And he probably doesn't know how to use a semi-colon."

She laughs. It's a pet hate of hers. "Seriously though, the baby is months away. You never know what could happen in the future. Why don't you go try the job out? If you don't like it, or change your mind you can always come back."

"I guess so," I concede.

"Good. I'm glad to hear it. So why are you still frowning?"

"I'm thinking of the usual things, I suppose. You know—moving from one country to another. All the red tape. All the little details. What to do with my apartment."

"Whether to keep it or not?" she asks.

"Well, I certainly don't want to move all my furniture to Italy. And things like dishes, linens, you know. Willa told me the place I'll be living is entirely furnished so what do I do with all my things? Should I sublet my place here? Should I put my things in storage? Should I keep the flat just in case ..."

"Well," she says reasonably, "why not do nothing for a couple of months until you decide for sure? I can keep everything ticking along for you."

"But everything has to be done quickly. I don't know if it's possible to do everything in the time I have."

"You're leaving that soon?" Star sounds surprised.

"Next week."

"Oh," she says and swallows hard.

Star is very vulnerable, and even though she tries hard not to show it, she can't bear it when the people she loves are not around her. When she first met Nikolai, she wanted me and Cindy to move into his mansion. 'It has like a hundred rooms,' was her justification. Both Cindy and I just shook our heads in wonder.

"Rome's not on the other side of the world, Star. We'll keep in touch—phone, email, Skype."

She nods sadly. "Of course, we will."

"And with the money I'll be making … I can afford to fly back to London any time I want, and you and Nikolai can come over for a dirty weekend too, right?"

"I'll miss you," she chokes out.

"And I'll miss you, Star," I say with feeling. Star and I have been through thick and thin together. Except for the time right after her first marriage to that dickhead, when I went to America to intern for Cosmo, we've never been apart.

"Right," she says with a sniff. "I'm going to stop being selfish. This is not about me. This is about you. Your big break." She makes a great effort to smile broadly. "I'm so, so, so happy for you, Rosa. This could be the best thing that ever happened to you. Other than the baby, of course. Obviously, I'll do whatever I can to help you."

The future stretches out, foreign, but exciting. "Thank you, my sweet Star."

"You said you have a week to move, right?"

"Signore Ricci, the owner, wants me to go to Rome immediately."

"Wow. So why you?"

"Uh huh."

She laughs. "Ooops … that didn't come across the way I meant it."

"No, it bloody didn't," I scold good-naturedly.

She giggles in the way that only Star can.

"From what I understand, Mr. Ricci's granddaughter is a fan of mine."

"His granddaughter?"

"Gina Ricci." I put on a melodramatic accent. "She adores every word I write apparently."

"Who knew you have such a big fan in Rome?"

I make a face. "I don't know. Doesn't it all sound a little fishy to you?"

"Fishy? In what way?"

"This offer coming totally so out of the blue right after I turn down Dante's offer of living in Rome with him. You know I don't believe in coincidences."

She shakes her head and looks at me strangely. "Stop being so paranoid. It's called good karma, Rosa. You deserve a break. Just enjoy it."

"It's probably the pregnancy. My head's never been the same since I found out. Okay, I'll just take it as a wonderful opportunity and enjoy every minute of it."

"That's my girl," she says, nodding and beaming at me.

We chat a few more moments and promise to get together for lunch the following day.

CHAPTER 8

Rosa

*T*he new opportunity really is a dream come true, and I look forward to it with great excitement, but I worry too. I've always been a writer, never an editor. Can I handle the responsibility? I can understand Italian and speak a passable amount, but is it enough to carry me in a competitive and professional environment where everyone will be speaking it?

Do I have any real idea what I am getting myself into?

Nevertheless, pure excitement and adrenaline keep me going as I clear out my desk and take care of any last-minute problems with the upcoming issue of *Mirabel.* After this it will be someone else's concern. I wonder who will replace me. Maybe Emily, or Willa could hire someone new.

Taking care of the practicalities of moving to a new country in one week turns out to not be as bad as I thought it would be. Especially as I decide to take Star's advice and keep the apartment for a few months more. Also, Star, being an author, simply made herself free for the whole week to help me out. To a lesser degree, Cindy and Raven pitched in too.

Between us and Star's shit-hot personal assistant we accomplish everything we need to. Notify the post office, pause all my different magazines, cancel the milk, and so on. I pack only what I think I'll need—laptop, clothing, some personal items. The magazine agrees to pay to ship anything I need. They have already rented a place not far from where I will be working. Someone from the publication will meet me at the airport to take me there.

I've traveled throughout Europe for weekend trips and vacations, but I've never lived anywhere but London. It's going to be hard to leave my familiar surroundings, my friends, and my family. When I tell my mother the good news, she puts the kettle on, and brings out the good brandy. We toast to my success and talk in her little yellow kitchen until my mother becomes very merry. As I am climbing the stairs up to my old bedroom, my mother touches my arm and tells me how proud she is of me. There are tears in her eyes. She says she will come over for the birth of the baby and stay as long as I need her.

On the last day Star and I are at my apartment while I try to decide what to take with me, what to leave behind, and what to ship. I don't know why I've left all this till practically the last moment. I usually make decisions easily. But not now, it seems. I dither over every item. "What about a bikini?" Star suggests, "it'll be really hot there now."

"I'm pregnant. Shouldn't I get a full suit?"

"Don't be silly. You'll look great in a bikini. I love to see the stomachs of pregnant women. I saved the pictures of Beyoncé with her big stomach."

I stare at her astonished. I know she loves babies, but saving an image of a pregnant woman. "Why on earth would you do that?"

She shrugs. "I just liked the whole thing. I just love a belly swollen with life. It's so beautiful."

I shake my head. "You can't tell me you actually think a big belly looks good."

She grins. "I think it's the most beautiful thing in the world. You wait until you see your belly growing. You'll change your mind then."

I cover the sides of my head with my hands. "I can't believe I'm talking about this when I'm such a mess. What if I've forgotten something really important?"

"Stop worrying, for heaven's sake," Star says. "It doesn't matter if you forget anything. I can have whatever you want shipped to you, and you know I'll be glad to take care of any little, last-minute details. Just bask in it!"

"Bask!"

"Yes. Enjoy the moment. Enjoy the fact that you're going to be living in one of the most romantic and cultured cities in the world."

"Bask, huh?"

"Bask, bask, bask."

"What if I fall flat on my face?"

"You won't, but if you do, you'll just get up, dust yourself off, and start again. You're magic, remember?"

I nod. "I am a bit nervous. It's such a big change."

"You'll be amazing. Just as you always have been."

"God, I wish I could pop you into my suitcase and take you with me."

She smiles, then bites her bottom lip. "You won't let anything change between us, will you, Rosa."

"Never."

CHAPTER 9

Rosa

https://www.youtube.com/watch?v=PxZHBxlwZBw
(Tell me when you will come,
Tell me when ... When ... When ...)

*T*he flight takes a little more than two hours. That's over two hours of butterflies flapping furiously in my tummy. I try to convince myself I'm being ridiculous. This is just another trip abroad. That I can always go back to England. Except it isn't. This is a life-changing trip. A new job. A new country. And I'm pregnant!

Finally, the pilot announces that we are landing.

I sail through customs, pick up my luggage, and enter the airport lobby. Looking around I immediately see a young woman holding a placard with my name on it.

"*Signorina* Gardener?" she asks.

I smile. "That's me. Rosa Gardener."

She smiles back. She has the whitest teeth I've ever seen, and pretty dimples at the corners of her mouth. "I am Carmela Moretti. I will be your secretary."

My eyes widen. Oh my! I've never had a secretary. "My secretary?" I can't help repeating.

She looks concerned. "If you don't object."

I rush to reassure. "No. No. Of course, I don't object." I grin again. "I've just never had a secretary before."

She flashes another dazzling smile. "In that case, I am very glad to meet you and very glad to be your first secretary. I have been asked to take you to your new home and show you around. I have done some shopping for you. I've filled your fridge with some essentials. Milk, cheese, ham and eggs. I also bought you some fresh bread from the bakery. I know English people like their tea so I got you a few varieties."

A great chunk of my nervousness leaves me. This is going to be a great adventure. I smile at her gratefully. "Wonderful. Thank you, Carmela."

After we collect my luggage—two large bags—Carmela leads me outside to the parking lot, and up to a bright yellow dung beetle Volkswagen. It has purple daisies painted on it. As if it is from the hippie era.

"I apologize," she mumbles.

"What for?" I ask.

"My car. It is very old, but I love it so much I can't bear to change it for another one."

I smile at her. "I think it is gorgeous, and a great indicator of real style when someone does their own thing."

Carmela beams at me and pops the trunk. We stow the luggage into it and climb into the car. The interior smells of vanilla and cinnamon.

"Now on to your new home … unless you'd like to stop anywhere first."

"No. Nowhere. I'm eager to see where I'll be staying."

Even though it's a Sunday afternoon, the streets are so crowded with fast moving vehicles, I'm glad Carmela's driving.

After a journey of many blocks, twists, and turns, we arrive in front of a pizzeria.

"We have arrived," Carmela says, and points to the top floor of the old two-story building. "That is where you'll be living." She turns to me. "That is, if you like it. We had to secure the rental very quickly, but if you don't like it we can change …" She sounds doubtful. "The good thing about it is I got you some of that terrible coffee in a bottle." She scrunches her face with disgust. "So if you don't like it you can always go down to the pizzeria for a proper coffee."

I gaze up at the intricate ancient plasterwork on the exterior of the building and fall in love with my new address. The whole idea of living above a pizzeria is incredibly romantic to me. Carmela parks the car and we get out. From inside the pizzeria comes the sound of loud Italian folk music. Carmela carries one of my suitcases, and I carry the other one.

"I love the smell of pizza," I say as I wait for Carmela to unlock the door at the side of the pizzeria.

"That's great since you're going to be smelling a lot of it." She realizes what she has said and hastens to add, "however, yours is the only apartment above the shop so you will have a lot of privacy."

We climb the narrow stone stairs and at the top she opens the door. I walk in, put my suitcase down, and glance around in awe. The flat is surprisingly beautiful—furnished much more expensively than any place I've ever lived. The floor is highly polished wood, the ceiling is lofty. Heavy drapes in mixed shades of blue and red cover the windows. The living room furniture, consisting of a sofa and two armchairs, look almost as comfortable as my own butter-soft sofa.

Carmela goes forward, opens a window, and turns to face me. "Well, what do you think?"

"It's perfect," I tell her softly. "I don't see how anyone would want to leave such a place. Just look at the view from the window!"

"I'm very happy that you're happy."

I laugh then. The first proper laugh since I found out about this job. Star was right. Everything will work out.

After Carmela leaves I go to the window and look out at the stunning view. The afternoon sun falls on the grey stone walls of the ancient Basilica making the majesty and beauty of the cathedral take my breath away. Laughter and the strains of Italian opera float up from the pizzeria. I breathe in the dry air of this unfamiliar land. I made the right decision. This is the place I'm meant to be.

It is all so perfect, it's like being in a dream.

The sudden ringing of my cell phone snaps me out of the moment of almost spiritual awareness and triggers a feeling of annoyance. However, it might be Carmela with something important to tell me, so I can't ignore it.

"Hello."

"It's me, Dante."

My heart stops beating. "How did you get my number?" I demand.

"I asked Star."

I can hardly believe it. "Star gave you my number?"

"You seem surprised."

"She's not supposed to."

"She gave you my number," he points reasonably.

"That's different," I say grumpily.

"Star thinks we'd make a great couple."

"Well, I don't."

"Don't hang up, please."

I clutch the phone hard. "Give me one good reason not to."

"I'm very good in bed," he drawls in his sexy voice that even now sends lovely little chills of excitement down my spine.

The fact that he can turn me on so easily irritates me. I can't allow him to get to me again. "I can't believe you just said that," I begin furiously. "Going to bed with you the first time only got me in trouble."

"But it was great, wasn't it?" Dante asks cheerfully.

It's hard to be angry with him when he sounds so happy. Yeah, playboy happy!

"Look, if you just called to boast about your sexual powers, I'm going to hang up."

"I called because I want to take you out for dinner."

"Why? Did you call some other woman and she turned you down?" I ask sourly.

He ignores my little jibe and says instead, "I know this nice little restaurant that serves to die for Roman dishes."

"No thanks. I think I'd rather die than go to dinner with you."

"The last time I heard such a categorical statement from you, you ended up in my bed," he shoots back.

I keep my voice cool. "I was inebriated the last time. I'm stone-cold sober right now."

"Then you have nothing to worry about."

"Has it ever crossed your mind that I don't want to have

dinner with you because I just plain don't enjoy your company?"

"No."

"Oh, my God. I give up. You're without doubt the most arrogant, vain, infuriating, irritating, and shallow man I have ever had the misfortune to come across."

"Will you come if I promise not to seduce you?" he asks cheekily.

"Are you capable of being in a room with a woman and not *try* to seduce her?"

"That's one of the things I like about you. So witty."

"You know, I really don't like you at all."

"Nevertheless, you are a stranger in a foreign land and you need to eat."

"I have bread and cheese."

"Come on, Rosa. We have to kiss and make up at some time. We have our child to think of. Say yes, and I'll send a taxi to pick you up," he says persuasively.

I should say no and hang up on him! I open my mouth to utter those exact words but instead find myself saying, "I really don't know why I am agreeing to have dinner with you. I'm sure I'll regret this decision."

"Rosa, your words are like arrows shot into my heart. But thanks for saying yes. The taxi will be there shortly, *bella*,"

"Don't call me—" The line goes dead.

I groan as I stare at my cell phone. Why, why does he have to be so damn irresistible? If he was not so ripped and delicious I might have been able to say no. However, in spite of my misgivings, I find myself more than a little excited about going out to dinner with him. There is something about him that goes beyond his good looks. I am also perfectly aware that I am deliberately rude and horrible to him because I don't want him to know just how much I like him. Still, he is right. He is the father of my child and I have to find some way of communicating with him that isn't completely made up of exchanging barbed insults.

"This isn't a date and he isn't your boyfriend!" I tell myself as I put my clothes away in the cupboards and drawers, but I find myself choosing a black, low-cut cocktail dress. A little cleavage never hurt a girl. I slip on a pair of black high heels and look at myself in the mirror. Not bad for a pregnant woman. I turn sideways and smooth the material over my belly. My pregnancy isn't showing yet. I try not to think of the future when my belly gets so big I have to wear those hideous maternity blouses. How Star can think that is attractive is beyond me. I'll just have to hope the nine months whizz past without me noticing too much.

The smell of pizza filtering up from the restaurant below causes my mouth to water as I sit waiting for the taxi. When I hear a horn blowing in the street below, I quickly open the window, and stick my head out. Waving at the taxi driver, I yell, *"Un minuto, signore."* I realize as I say those words that if I'm going to live in Italy, I'll have to learn to speak Italian properly. I just heard how awful my pronunciation is.

"Yes, I wait for you," the driver shouts back in heavily accented English, as though he fears I am going to continue butchering his language.

I grab my matching black clutch purse and keys to my new home off the small decorative table and hurry out of my apartment. As I reach the street, I pass the window of the pizzeria. A fat Italian man is twirling pizza dough in his meaty raised hand. He smiles at me as he throws the spinning dough into the air and catches it.

To be honest, I feel a little like a bit of pizza dough that Dante is tossing into the air. I hope he plans to catch me before I hit the ground hard.

"No need to rush, *signorina*, I wait for pretty English lady all day," the driver says as I hurry to his cab.

God, all Italian men are alike. "Thank you," I say and climb into the back seat. "I don't know the address ..."

"Don't worry. Dante gives me address. He waits for you," he says with a smile.

Yeah, like a hawk ready to swoop down on a chicken. Well, forewarned is forearmed.

CHAPTER 10

Rosa
https://www.youtube.com/watch?v=R3ihv5ateWw
Another you
(Un'Altra Te)

he ride calms my nerves. Rome is so beautiful and so full of architectural marvels it's hard to be anything but impressed. On every street and corner there is a statue, a gorgeous fountain, or a building of note to look at. I don't want to be angry and shrewish tonight. I will be firm and polite. I'm not going to sleep with him or change my mind about all the decisions I have made. I have a great job and I can take care of my baby without his help.

Tonight, I will be adult and mature.

The little restaurant is on a side street so narrow I fear the taxi is going to scrape the sides of the buildings.

I'm surprised to see Dante lounging against the front of the restaurant, waiting for me. He's wearing a camel sport coat over a maroon shirt with khaki pants and light brown loafers. If it looks like a playboy, dresses like a playboy, and talks like a playboy it must be one. God, why did it have to be him? If it was anyone else I could have kept my sanity.

He smiles slowly and walks over to open the door for me. Taking my hand as I exit the taxi, he kisses me lightly on the cheek. The scent of his aftershave fills my nostrils and makes my knees go weak. Hell, it must be the hormones, but I actually want to lick him.

"You look good enough to eat," he murmurs in my ear.

I almost swoon. To cover it I abruptly pull away and pretend to be irritated he sent a taxi to pick me up. "You sent a taxi to pick me up," I say coldly.

"I'm sorry, *bella*, I was busy." A devilish glint comes into his eyes. "But you can be sure it will be me who takes you home tonight."

"Busy with another naked girl in your suite?" I ask, arching my eyebrows as if the idea didn't make my stomach turn with raw jealousy.

"No, the only girl I want to see naked is you."

"I thought you weren't going to try to seduce me."

Dante's face breaks into a smile that goes all the way to his whiskey eyes making them sparkle with amusement. "Sorry. Force of habit."

I scowl at him.

"Let's start again, huh? Thank you for coming, Rosa. I hate to eat alone."

"I'm sure you never eat alone."

"That's true," he admits, before suavely slipping his hand down to the small of my back and turning me towards the restaurant. "Come, I have a table reserved for us."

"What about the taxi? You haven't paid him?"

"Oh, he knows I'm good for the fare. I use him regularly. Besides he'll be picking us up after our dinner and taking us back—," Dante says as he opens the door to the restaurant for me.

I catch his eyes. "To our different addresses."

His eyes glint. "You're the boss."

I glance around at the seven tables, six of which are occupied by well-dressed couples.

"*Signore* Dante!" the maître d', a dapper little man, cries gaily, as he hurries toward us with quick clownish steps. "How wonderful to see you again. And who is this beautiful *Signorina* you have graced us with tonight?"

Dante looks down at me indulgently. "Yes, you could say she is an English rose that England has lost to Rome."

I blink in confusion at the flowery praise.

"Ah, but you are a lucky man, *Signore* Dante. Lucky man," he says, looking at me with admiring eyes, but he is so good at his job, his gaze does not leave the realms of his job description. He's just making his customers feel good. Dante for choosing a beautiful woman and me for being beautiful. "This way, please. Your table is ready."

"A bottle of my usual wine, please, Sergio," Dante says, as Sergio snaps my napkin open with a flick of his wrist and lays it on my lap.

"Yes, at once," Sergio replies with a nod.

"I'll just have bottled water, please," I say.

"Of course, *Signorina*," he says with a bow, and leaves.

"I'm surprised he speaks English," I say, smoothing my napkin. In the low restaurant lighting he looks like he has been carved out of hard wood by some great sculptor. My fingers itch to touch the hard planes of his face.

"He knows that you are English. It would be disrespectful for him to speak Italian unless he was sure you understood."

"That's not been my experience. You sure you're not the owner of this place?"

"Owning restaurants is not my thing."

"Pardon me, I forgot your thing is sweeping women off their feet."

"My only interest is in sweeping you off your feet," Dante murmurs, his voice like dark velvet.

"You're doing it again," I say tightly.

"I love a feisty girl," Dante says. "Make-up sex with you is going to be fantastic."

I swallow the sharp words that are on the tip of my tongue. *Play nice*, I tell myself. *He brought you to this wonderful, romantic restaurant, so enjoy yourself. Don't let him get under your skin. You can always duke it out with him later.*

"Do all Italian men think only about sex?"

"I can't speak for others, but I'm hard enough to chip wood just looking at you," he drawls smoothly, as a waiter brings a bottle of red wine and begins to open it.

"Maybe you should take your palm and go to the men's room."

Dante flashes a mischievous smile. "Don't you think I already did that before I came?"

My eyes widen at the casual confession. Really, this man is irredeemable. I want to kick him under the table. He brings every topic of conversation effortlessly back to the issue of sex.

Dante swirls the wine in his glass, sniffs it and nods his approval to the waiter, who then who fills my glass a third full. When his glass is filled, Dante raises it. "A toast to your new job and your life in Rome!"

The angry thoughts slip out of my mind as I raise my glass and touch it lightly to his. His lips curve upwards. How can any man be this charming? And that brings me to my next question. What the hell am I doing here with him? I'm falling for his dark, handsome looks and Italian charm like I did the first time we met. Didn't I learn my lesson then?

Dante raises his hand with his beautifully manicured nails and motions to the waiter. I take a tiny sip of the wine. It is very smooth. Then put it away regretfully, and reach for the water.

"*Carpaccio* and *osso bucco* for both of us, please," Dante tells the waiter.

It is only then I realize we have not been given any menus. "Excuse me. Did you just order for me?" I ask incredulously.

Dante looks at me, one eyebrow raised. "You are in Roma, Rosa. You must try the specialty of the house. They are actually famous for it. It's cross-cut veal shanks braised with vegetables in a white wine broth. I don't believe I've ever had a better *osso bucco* anywhere else in Italy. People come from all over the world just for this dish."

Ignoring Dante, I address the waiter directly. "I will have the carpaccio, but not the osso bucco. Do you have salmon?"

His eyes dart over to Dante. Dante just shrugs so he turns back to me, and nods. "Of course, *Signorina*."

"Good. I'll have that," I say decisively.

"I love a rebellious woman," Dante says. His eyes glitter with some unspoken promise.

I break my breadstick with more force than necessary. "Well, I don't like men who order for me."

He leans back and regards me curiously.

"What?" I ask aggressively.

"You don't want me to seduce you. You don't want me to mention sex. What would you like to talk about?"

I clear my throat and lift up my glass of water. "It's really hot here, isn't it?"

He grins. "This is nothing. Wait till August. It gets so fucking hot my balls stick to my legs."

I nearly spray my mouthful of water all over the table. I swallow it hurriedly, and of course, it goes the wrong way and gives me a coughing fit. Dante stands up and comes over to rub my back. His hand is warm and firm and, quite frankly, addictive. The coughing stops and strange things start happening in my belly. I use my napkin to dab at the corners of my eyes.

"Thanks. I'm fine now," I tell him with as much dignity as I can. I can feel the eyes of all the other diners on me. I take another sip of water while he returns to his seat.

"Apparently, body parts are off the list too," he remarks.

I say the first thing that comes into my head. "If restaurants are not your thing, what is it you do for a living?"

He shrugs nonchalantly. "I don't work for a living."

"Must be nice," I say sarcastically.

"Ah, you are one of those people who have been brainwashed into believing that hard work equals respectability. That a life without work is somehow wasted or useless."

"I would be extremely bored if I didn't work."

"How boring your life must be if it is only in work that you get your utmost satisfaction."

Before I can answer him, the waiter brings a large platter of raw beef cut so thin the slices are almost transparent. It is finished with arugula leaves and shaved parmesan. The leaves glisten with the olive oil drizzled on them. The waiter leaves the platter in the middle of the table and grinds pepper over it. I watch Dante squeeze lemon onto it.

"*Buon appetito,*" he says with a smile.

"Same to you," I say and slip the silky bit of meat and leaves into my mouth.

"Good?"

"Very," I say honestly. We finish the platter in record time, and I lie back in my chair as our plates are cleared away.

The waiter returns almost immediately with miniature bowls of what looks like tomato soup.

"Is this tomato soup?"

"It's a slow-roasted tomato bisque. They do it exceptionally well here, and I wanted you to try it," Dante explains.

I take a spoonful of the velvety liquid. It is rich and delicious on my tongue. "Mmm ... very tasty."

Dante grins. "Do you know they call it *pomme D'amo*ur because it is supposed to be an aphrodisiac?"

"As though you need something to spark your sex drive," I scoff.

"I was trying to spark yours," Dante replies.

I look unimpressed. "Then you better ask them to bring a huge pail of it."

"I'm mortally wounded."

"That will be the day. Your skin is thicker than a rhino's."

He throws his head back and laughs. "I like you."

"Well, I can't say the same to you."

He leans closer and instantly my breath hitches. "I don't need you to like me, *bella*. I just need you to want me."

I put the spoon down. "I'm never sleeping with you again, Dante. I thought I made that very clear."

He reaches out and lets his fingers brush my cheek. I want to jerk away, but I can't. It feels too good. "You have a true English rose complexion. I don't think I have ever met anyone with such fine skin."

"I'm not sleeping with you, Dante. I really, really mean it."

"I know you do," he says softly, as he gazes deep into my eyes. I feel like a hypnotized rabbit. I can't look away. He removes his hand and his lips curve upwards. "Now eat your bisque."

I tear my gaze away from him and look down into the thick, red liquid in my bowl. The next time I raise my head is when I have got my heartbeat back to normal. I lean back to let the waiter clear away our bowls.

Another waiter brings our main dishes. In front of me he sets a plate with saffron rice and a narrow slice of salmon on it, but the truly delicious smell comes from Dante's plate.

"Enjoy, *bella*," Dante says.

He cuts a piece of meat, spears it with his fork, and lifts it toward my mouth. I pause a moment before opening my mouth. "You have to try," he says softly. I open my mouth and he slips the meat in. God, he was right. It is to die for. He stares into my eyes as I chew the juicy piece of meat.

"Is it good?"

"It's exquisite. I really like it," I admit, impressed with how good it is. I was expecting the normal Italian restaurant fare of veal parmigiana and spaghetti bolognese. This is an unexpected and delightful change. I decide to bring mum here when she comes to visit.

'You can still change your order. I'll have mine kept warm and brought out again."

"No, it's okay."

He grins. "Want mine?"

I stare at him in surprise. "No, I don't want yours. It's my own fault for being so stubborn."

"Shall we share it?"

I smile at him. For the first time, I feel close to him. Maybe he's not such a bad guy, after all.

So that's what we do. We share everything. Dante keeps the conversation light and easy and I actually start to enjoy his company and the intelligence that he mostly hides behind his shallow Casanova exterior.

An hour later, I drop my napkin onto the table. "I can't eat another mouthful of this dessert!" I say reluctantly pushing away the small dish with a third of the portion of goose egg *zabaglione* still on my glass. "But it was all very, very delicious, Dante. Thank you."

"I am glad you enjoyed it. This is just your first night in Italy. Just think of all the new experiences you will have."

I tilt my head to the side. "Yeah?"

"And probably some old experiences too," he murmurs, his eyes sliding down to my breasts.

I feel hot color rush up my face.

"On that note, I think I should take you back to your apartment. It's been a long day for you, and you must be tired."

"Yes, I'm tired."

Dante pulls out his cell phone and pushes a single button. "Salvatore, come pick us up," he says and then puts his phone back inside his pocket.

Then he waves for the waiter and hands him his credit card.

The taxi is waiting by the time we walk out of the restaurant into the cool night air.

"That was fast," I say. "He wasn't waiting around the corner or something, was he?"

"Maybe," Dante says casually, as he holds the taxi door open.

"Bona sera," Salvatore says.

"To the *Signorina*'s apartment," Dante instructs.

"He remembers where I live?"

"Of course."

The ride back seems shorter than the drive to the restaurant. But then returning home always seems to take less time than going to a destination. We ride with the windows down and Dante takes it upon himself to point out the different sights. Rome at night is intoxicatingly beautiful.

"Oh, we're here already," I exclaim, recognizing the pizza restaurant as the taxi slows down.

Dante gets out of the taxi and comes around to open my door.

Having a man behave in such a courtly way is unusual to me. I have always believed that I am more than capable of opening my doors and I honestly didn't want any man to do that for me. And yet, here I am impressed that Dante is pulling the gentlemanly routine.

I get out and turn to him. "It was a very nice meal, Dante. Thank you. I think I am going to enjoy exploring the restaurants in Rome."

"How about a cup of coffee?"

I bite my lip. "It's late, Dante."

"You're not going to deny me one little cup of coffee?"

"I only have instant."

His face screws up. "My favorite type," he lies blatantly.

"Okay, but don't make me regret it," I say with a sigh.

CHAPTER 11

Rosa

I watch him lean back into the taxi and hand the driver some bills.

"Buono notte," the driver yells before he drives off.

"Do you like your apartment?" Dante asks as we start walking.

"Yes, it is lovely and the magazine has stocked it with essentials too," I say as we go past the pizza restaurant that still seems to be buzzing with life and activity. "I definitely have to try one of their pizzas. Even though I am stuffed, that smell is doing something to me."

"Pizza will make you fat," Dante says as we climb the stairs.

"Oh God, don't talk about getting fat. I am going to have to turn all the mirrors around when my belly starts growing. I won't even want to look at myself."

"Oh, yes you will. You'll pat your stomach and feel the life growing inside and get emotional knowing you are going to be the best mother in the world," Dante says as I push the door to my apartment.

"Oh yeah? And how do you know so much about it?"

"I've been reading *Parenting Magazine*."

I laugh. "No, you haven't. And I know for a fact they don't have articles about expectant mothers in *Playboy*."

Dante smiles as he looks around the room. "Now serve me some of that terrible coffee of yours."

"My God, you Italians all have such a snobbish attitude towards coffee," I tease.

"It's the rest of the world that doesn't know how to appreciate good coffee."

I roll my eyes. "Whatever."

He sits at my kitchen table and talks to me while I make the coffee.

"Here we are," I say, holding one mug out to him. His fingers touch mine, and suddenly, the atmosphere changes. The air becomes thick. For a second I can only stare at him blankly as his eyes darken, then I rush to fill the molten silence.

"Taste it, then."

He takes a sip and his mouth turns down at the corners. "Undrinkable," he declares, putting the mug down.

I laugh at his expression. "Coffee in my kitchen overlooking that cathedral has to be worth something."

"It is," he says softly. "I wouldn't let that disgusting stuff pass my lips under any other circumstances."

"Dante." I say putting down my mug. "I keep thinking how extraordinarily lucky I am to get this awesome, once-in-a-lifetime job here in this beautiful city, but the thing is I'm not exactly the luckiest person I know."

The room becomes very quiet. Dante looks at me steadily, but says nothing.

"You … er … don't happen to know the owner of the magazine, do you?"

"Not really," he says evasively.

My eyes narrow. "Not really? What the hell does that mean? Do you or don't you know him?" I demand.

"We met at a party once," he admits.

"I see. Hmmm … so you didn't recommend me for the job?"

"Not to him."

I blink, then my jaw drops. "Oh my God! Oh, my God."

"I just mentioned your name, Rosa."

"You big asshole. You asked his granddaughter, didn't you?" I jump up and begin pacing. "Oh, gross! Just gross."

"You seem very upset. Why?"

I whirl around and face him. "Why? How can you even ask me that? You asked your ex-girlfriend to hire the woman carrying your child. Can you not see how fucked up that is?"

He shrugs. "No. It's not fucked up at all. I want you and my child close to me and believe me, this is nothing. I would have done anything to get both of you here."

I start pacing again. "You're mad. I'm shocked she agreed. What kind of woman does that?"

"Why wouldn't she? Yes, we were lovers once, but we aren't anymore. It's simply an exchange of favors. She does this for me and another day I might be able to do something for her."

I stop pacing and glare at him. "So she has never even read my work, has she?"

"Well, yes. After I spoke to her, she read your work. Obviously, you wouldn't have got the job if you had been useless."

I run my hands through my hair. "Oh, shit. This is so embarrassing. And I thought I got the job on merit alone."

"Does it really matter? You have the job."

"Yes, it matters," I howl. "I have this dream job that I thought I got because of my ability, but now I find out I snagged it because someone I had sex with asked the owner to hire me! Do you realize how sleazy that makes me feel?"

"Okay, I pulled some strings to land you the job. You should be thanking me instead of getting angry."

"Thanking you. I am going to have to go into the office every day and face people who probably know I got the job only because I slept with Dante, the playboy!"

"Grow up, Rosa. When you accepted that job you did so because you believed in yourself and your ability to do it. That has not changed. The reality is life is a series of unfair advantages. You had a lot more advantages than a girl growing up in an African village, for example. What is important is how you handle the fate you're given!"

I can't believe he's saying this. I stare at him incredulously. He sits gazing back at me. Totally sexy, masculine, confident, without a care in the world, and utterly unaware of the rage he has ignited in me.

"God, you're the first man who's made me feel like slapping you really hard," I mutter.

He arches one eyebrow as his mouth tilts with amusement. "Really?"

"Absolutely," I say between clenched teeth

"It is a sexual thing?"

I throw my hands up in the air. How do you deal with a man like this? "No, it is not a sexual thing."

He starts walking towards me. "Are you sure?"

"Of course, I'm sure. It's pure fury."

He stops in front of me. "Ah. What a shame."

Even though I am bursting with anger, his nearness has a strange effect on

me so I turn away. My plan is to put as much distance as possible between us. But as I start walking toward the window, my hand gets caught by his. I whirl around and the words on my tongue die at the look in his eyes.

Smug bastard. He is so sure he is going to bed me.

I don't know why he always has this effect on me, but I stop thinking. Either I go weak at the knees, or I become a bitter shrew. At that moment, red hot rage slams into my head. I do what I have never done before. I wrench my hand out of his grasp, take a few steps away from him and charge, using my head like a battering ram.

I crash into his abs.

Fuck! It is like crashing my head into a brick wall. It's possible I broke my neck or did it lasting injury, but that doesn't stop me. Fueled by frustration, rage, and a hidden sadness. I kick his shin so hard with the sharp end of my shoes he stumbles backwards.

But I'm not finished.

With a cry of fury, I launch myself at him. His hands come around me. It's almost a protective gesture, but I register only the fact of falling on him is turning me on. I can feel his cock hard and thick against my stomach. With all my might, I try to pull away from him, but suddenly, he has me trapped between him and the wall. I lift my hand to slap him. He catches it easily.

"Bastard," I yell, and swing the other one wildly towards his face, but he catches that one just as effortlessly. He grips both my wrists in his hand and takes them over my head.

We stare at each other. I'm panting hard.

"I hate you," I snarl.

"No, you don't. You just hate that you cannot control the way you feel about me."

"Yes, I do. You smug, selfish, shallow, arrogant, womanizing jerk."

He leans down so that his face is very close to mine. "Yes, I am all those things, but you are also carrying *my* child. It will be a cold day in hell before I walk away from that responsibility. Neither of us are free agents anymore, Rosa. We owe it to the life we created to get on."

"If your idea of getting on is having sex with me whenever you feel like it, you can forget it right now, because I am *never* having sex with you again."

"I want our child to have all the advantages we can give him. I say 'we' because I want to marry you and give the child my name."

"Again with that? Don't you get it? I don't want to marry you."

"Why not?"

"Because of all the reasons I mentioned earlier. I don't want a selfish bastard for a husband who cheats on me. I've been around your type in London. They go from one girl to the next, never leaving their wives but constantly cheating on those sad women. I don't want that type of marriage. Sooner or later, you'll break my heart. To put it nicely you are too gorgeous a man to marry."

He looks deep into my eyes. "Sometimes what you see on the outside is not what is really on the inside. Sometimes the men who seem to be good and loyal are the ones who secretly need the high of cheating on their wives. I'm an open book. I slept with many women, but never cheated on

65

anyone. I was a free agent. When we marry I will no longer be one."

"Exactly. You will get bored and you'll be itching to try new flesh."

"Have you ever thought that maybe I've had all the flesh I want? You don't crave for something that has been plentiful. You crave for the rare thing."

I stare at him, mesmerized by his words. I so much want to believe it. "Talk is cheap," I whisper.

"Then let me prove it to you."

"That sounds like a win-win situation for you. If you make it because you like being married you win, if you decide it's not for you, which is the more likely scenario, you say sorry and walk away. But I get my heart broken."

"You never struck me as a coward, Rosa. What's the point of living if you are never going to take a chance on anything that looks like it might bring you hurt?"

"I don't care. I am not marrying you."

"Do you want me to get down on one knee like they do in those corny movies?"

"No."

"No, you don't want me to get down on one knee? Or no you don't want to marry?"

"Both. Please, don't ask me again! You are not marriage material … not for me, anyway."

Suddenly I feel Dante's lips pressing against mine. I feel my resistance melting. He stops kissing me and raises his head to look into my eyes. Immediately I push my hands against his chest. He kisses me again. This time his tongue slips into my mouth. His kiss saps all the strength out of my arms. I stop pushing against him and give in to the tremendous passion of his kiss.

I find myself clutching and pulling him closer to my breast instead of pushing him away. I feel him responding to my hard nipples nudging his chest.

He raises his head.

"We shouldn't," I mumble weakly as I attempt one last effort to resist him when we break our embrace.

"Oh, yes we should," Dante says as he reaches behind me and grabs the tab of my dress' zipper. "Let me see this beautiful body that drives me wild," he adds as he pulls down the zipper.

I hold the front of my dress over my breasts as Dante zips it all the way down.

He shakes his head. "Don't hide your candy from me."

"You are such a pervert," I say even as I let go of the front of my dress. It drops to the floor to form a pool of black shimmering silk in front of my black high heels.

Dante takes a step back. "Lovely. I love all your body, but your breasts are perfection," he says as he leans his head down and takes one of my hard nipples into his mouth.

I sigh loudly as he runs his tongue around my nipple before caressing the top of it with the tip of his warm, wet tongue.

"You are a very wicked man, Dante," I mutter, as I run my fingers through his thick dark hair.

CHAPTER 12

Dante

https://www.youtube.com/watch?v=e-Sq2-zvpXE
Tennessee Whiskey

J've had to pretend to be unaffected all this time. To banter with her as if she is just another sexual conquest when all I want to do is open her thighs and consume her. In the taxi, I had the fucking devil on my shoulder tempting and urging me to grab her ankles, open her up, and take her right there on Salvatore's back seat.

But I clenched my hands into fists and held back.

No, the last thing I want to do is frighten her with the kind of intensity I feel. When you land a very big fish you reel it in slowly and steadily. You resist its thrashes, while you continue to pull it in. Tiring it, making it understand you are the greater force. She can struggle as much as she likes, but I will endure. Nothing can turn me away from my purpose.

This woman is mine, and no man will ever touch her again.

I feast my eyes on her naked body. It feels like years since I touched and tasted her. Her body is exactly as I remembered. Every plane, every creamy curve. Perfect.

I pull a pink nipple into my mouth and she moans. The sound drives me wild. I suck the hard pebble and she arches her back and pushes into me. I smell the sweet thick scent of her arousal. Uncontrollable lust rips through me. Like a caveman I want to mate. I want my cock inside her.

But I'm here for the long haul.

I pull my mouth away from her nipple and look into her face. Her big, beautiful eyes are glazed with desire. "These breasts are mine," I growl, grabbing them both and pinching the nipples. "I never want another man's hands to touch them. Do you understand?"

She inhales sharply, but she nods.

I bend my head and lick her soft skin. Slowly, I travel downwards. I can't wait to get between her legs, but I try not to race there. I take my time. Kissing, licking, caressing on my way downwards. "One day when I do this I will hear our child's heartbeat," I say as I pause at her belly.

I lick her belly button with the tip of my tongue and her whole body tenses. Yes, she is exactly as I remember her to be. I place both my hands on the insides of her thighs, pull them apart, and look at the cleft between her legs. Her clit is swollen and sticking out from her lips. The tip is white. The whole area is wet and glistening. She's been like this for a long time.

"Oh God!" she cries out as I push my tongue between her lips and taste her sweet honey again. She grabs handfuls of my hair and pulls my face against her crotch.

I lose it then. I start eating her like a starving man.

"Yes, yes. Oh yes!" she groans as her body jerks with the waves

GEORGIA LE CARRE

of pleasure that sweep through her. Her body starts trembling.
I know the signs. She's about to climax. I tongue fuck her as
she hunches into my face. When I feel her about to go over, I
suck her clit hard. She screams and gushes her juices into my
mouth, onto my face, and throat. I lap her juices hungrily.

She is still panting hard when I stand and lift her into
my arms.

"Dante," she protests.

I don't respond. I can't. I am so hard and horny I can't talk. I
turn and carry my property from the kitchen towards the
door that obviously leads to her bedroom. I lay her on top of
the bed, kick off my shoes, and start to undo my belt. She
watches me drag down my pants, and rip away my shirt.

I'm engulfed by a sense of possession. I have never felt such a
thing before. As I watch her laid out naked, her legs askew,
waiting for me, I feel pride. This is my woman. All mine. The
sooner she understands it the better.

I press down on top of her soft curves. Her eyes gaze into
mine. Open and vulnerable.

"Tell me you want me," I tell her.

"No," she says.

I kiss her. I kiss her passionately until her fingers rise up to
wind into my hair, until she is breathless.

"Tell me you want me. Say it," I order.

"I want you," she mutters, but reluctantly.

I plunder her mouth again. This time I hook her tongue with
mine, take it into my mouth, and suck it hard until her body
feels boneless beneath mine.

I lift my head. Her eyes are half-closed and her pupils are
almost as large as her irises.

"Tell me you want me," I command again.

"I want you," she says breathlessly, eagerly.

"Tell me you need my cock inside your pretty pussy."

"I need your cock inside my pretty pussy," she repeats, and wriggles her hips to encourage me.

"Good. Now tell me you're mine. You belong to me."

She stares into my eyes, like a rabbit hypnotized by headlights. "I'm yours. I belong to you."

Her words spoken without shame are music to my ears. Now I just have to claim her.

I hold her face. "You ready?" I ask.

Biting her bottom lip, she nods.

Without another word, I push the thick mushroom-shaped head of my cock into her tight pussy.

Her eyes widen at the size of the intrusion. "Oh fuck!" she gasps, and I drive my cock deeper inside her. She's so hot and wet, I nearly come.

"That's right, baby, oh fuck! This is what you are going to take inside you every day for the rest of your life," I growl in her ear as I drive my aching dick all the way in.

"Oh, God," she cries as I ram my cock all the way in. But it's not enough for me. I want deeper.

"You like me to be rough with you, baby?"

Her eyes snap up to mine. A greedy, wicked smile spreads on her face. "I want it all," she whispers.

I grab one of her thighs, throw it over my shoulder, and slam all the way in. She screams then. The sound drives me crazy. I've been wanting to hear it ever since that first night. I look down and she is spread open wide and taking all of me inside her. I pull out a little, and reaching between us, rub her beautiful engorged clit.

She shudders with pleasure.

Buried deep inside her I circle that swollen bud relentlessly. Her hips buck as her cream seeps out and flows down to her puckered ass. Yeah, I'll have that too. Not today. But soon. That's mine to claim as well.

Her pussy starts clenching tightly around me, squeezing my cock. She jerks her hips restlessly. "Don't stop, please," she begs.

I start slamming into her, slapping her little clit, making her cry out. Her little pussy milks my cock with its clenching movements, and I completely lose track of time. It could have been a minute, or an hour later when I hear her scream and feel her wrap her other leg around my waist as she experiences her second orgasm. This one is wild. The force of it makes her eyes roll back.

Watching it is too much for me. I lose my fucking mind. No longer able to hold back, I come with a roar. I continue to pump my cock violently into her, spewing hot cum inside her sweet cunt.

"That was heaven," she says.

I lazily move my cock in and out of her as I caress her soft skin. I want to carry on. I could fuck her all night, but I won't. I know she has had a long day. I pull out of her, and watch my cum drip out of her. I move to climb out of bed.

"Where are you going?" she asks, her hand rising up to stop me.

"Sleep. I'll be back tomorrow."

"I'm not your fuck toy," she says angrily.

I smear my cum all over her pussy and her stomach. It's my way of marking her. "Yes you are. You are my fuck toy, my woman, my lover, the receptacle of my cum. I want to stay here and fuck you all night, but you have a new job, and tomorrow is your first day at work. You need the rest."

"Stay. I only need to close my eyes for a second," she mumbles. Her eyelids are already drooping as fatigue takes over. It's been a long day for her and she's pregnant.

"I will not let you go, Rosa. You, or my child."

She smiles softly in her sleep when I kiss her mouth.

CHAPTER 13

Rosa
https://www.youtube.com/watch?v=T2H5D58kAd0

J wake up before my alarm clock rings. One moment I'm fast asleep and dead to the world, and the next I've jerked bolt upright like something from a horror movie, leapt out of bed, and sprinting toward the bathroom. All kinds of images from last night of Dante and I come to me as I brush my teeth, but I push them away ruthlessly.

After my shower, I dress quickly in my red power suit. I stand in front of the mirror and look at myself. Especially, now that I know the route by which this job became mine, I am more determined than ever to prove how good I can be at this job. I check my phone and see that Cindy has already left me a good luck message with a funny GIF of a baby blowing kisses.

Carmela showed me yesterday how easy it is for me to walk to work if I set off early armed with my map. I know I will make it in time even if I lose my way once or twice. I slip my red shoes into my bag, and get into my trainers. No point having the heels of my good shoes ruined in the cracks between the cobblestones.

Locking my door, I glance into the pizzeria as I walk past it. I expect it to be empty, but to my surprise it is already buzzing with activity. One of the men makes a beckoning motion towards me. I hesitate, but he moves his hands even more vigorously. Since I am very early, I push open the door and go in.

The man turns out to be a young waiter called Enzo. He and Luigi, one of the dishwashers, insist on serving me a strong coffee from a shiny monster of a machine. It is so thick it coats my tongue like honey. They offer me cone-shaped pastry dusted in sugar that they tell me comes from the best bakery in Rome, but even the sight of it makes me want to hurl, so I politely refuse. Like every Italian man I have ever met, both lads are outrageous flirts who are unashamedly curious about me. Who am I? Where am I from? How long am I staying? I am only allowed to leave after I promise to come in for a pizza sometime during the week.

The morning air is fresh and the walk is invigorating.

Surrounded by intricate ancient stone work, and gothic spires, I feel exhilarated and excited about my new job. Of course, I hate it that Dante intervened for me, but he is right. I've been given a golden opportunity, I can either sulk about it, or go all out and prove that I can do the job and do it well.

Carmela is waiting for me outside the grey building *Mirabel* occupies. She greets me with a big smile. "Ready to take on Rome's fashion world?"

"Oh, I don't know about that. I am a bit nervous. I've never been an editor, and to attempt it in a different country … I could fail in a really spectacular way," I say as I quickly exchange my trainers for my good shoes.

"Or you could succeed in a really spectacular way," she quips.

Her smile is sincere and I smile back at her gratefully. I am glad she's on my team. "Thank you, Carmela. You are very sweet. Now if only the rest of the staff are as friendly."

"Actually, everyone is waiting to welcome the new English editor."

"You're sure about that?" Somehow, I find it quite hard to believe her, but I don't say anything. I know everybody would have gone mad back in *Mirabel* London if some stranger from Italy had swooped in and stolen the top job from under their noses.

She shrugs. "It's a good group. We get along very well."

Carmela holds open the door for me and I'm instantly impressed by the building's interior. It looks like a church that has been transformed into a gallery for modern art.

"Different, isn't it?"

"Not at all what I expected," I agree.

We cross the reception to the elevator. "Wait till you see our floor. I think you'll be impressed."

"I already am," I say, looking around me at the colorful pieces of art decorating the walls.

She pushes the button for our floor. The first thing I notice when we step out of the elevator is the near silence. I expected it to be something like *Mirabel* London where there's always a buzz of mingled voices and the usual sounds of a busy publishing enterprise—printers, the clacking of keyboards, people talking over each other. Here it is as quiet as a temple.

I turn to Carmela, puzzled.

"That's everyone's reaction," Carmela tells me with a grin. "It's the special walls and ceilings, designed to absorb sound."

I shake my head. "After the constant chaos at *Mirabel*—this is just … unbelievable."

"Come on. I'll show you to your office, and then we'll make the rounds."

We walk down a glass corridor. All the while curious heads, men and women in their twenties and thirties, keep lifting up to peek at us. Finally, Carmela opens a door in front of us. "Your office is this way." She steps in front of me, takes a turn to the right, and makes an expansive gesture with one hand. "What do you think?"

I look around in awe. At the large kidney-shaped desk with a thick glass top, the curving cream sofa, the two easy chairs, and the conference table with eight chairs. This is Italian style at its best. My new office is at least twice the size of Willa's room back in London. "My goodness. It's so big."

"Nice, huh?"

"Nice? Wow. I love the furniture. I certainly never expected an office that could fit a conference table."

Carmela laughs. "Good. Rosella, the person you are taking over from, liked to hold all staff meetings in her office where she served pastries, coffee, tea, hors d'oeuvres, and even dim sum. Of course, you might want to do things differently."

I grin. "No. I think it's a brilliant tradition."

Carmela grins back. "Are you ready for the tour?"

From then on it's a whirlwind of people's faces and names, all blending together. She shows me to a large production studio where a lot of in-house visual content is created. Full of excitement I go from department to department. The Green Room, where celebrities or talent wait before participating in a photo or video shoot. The large styling area, the newsroom with all the TVs so that everybody can follow breaking news or cover awards, the kitchen and bar areas for when deadlines are approaching and staff work around the clock. I can hardly believe how big and glamorous *Mirabel*'s Rome arm is.

With the tour over, Carmela introduces me to the editorial staff. I'd worried how everyone would react to having a new editor, but so far, there doesn't seem to be any problem. Everyone is courteous and friendly. Maybe if they knew how I got the job they wouldn't be so cooperative, but at the moment all is hunky dory.

By the time I've met everyone and understood what they all do, it's nearly time for lunch.

"Ready for a break?" Carmela asks.

"Am I ever!"

Carmela takes over and introduces me to her favorite restaurant in the area.

"I've been wondering," I say as we step inside a small intimate café where painted butterflies decorate the walls, "how your English is so perfect."

Carmela smiles. "I went to the San Diego State University for my bachelor of arts degree in English. I am working my way up. One day I plan to become the editor of a magazine too."

I give her a big smile. "I think you'll make a great editor one day. Thank you for making it so easy for me today."

"My job is to help you."

*B*ack at my office, I drop into my black leather chair and try to assimilate and absorb what I've learned, as well as collate everything that goes into the magazine. I'm also supposed to write the editorial piece of the month. I buzz Carmela. I ask her to bring me copies of the magazine for the past six months. In a couple of minutes she enters my office carrying the stack.

After she leaves I pick up one of the copies and flick through it. The quality surprises me. The paper is much thicker than those used by Mirabel in England. Of course that has to do with money from advertisers. As I slowly go through the pages to get a feel for it, I'm further impressed by how darned good the magazine is. Suddenly, I feel very lucky to have landed the job—thanks to Dante or not.

As I look through the six publications, I notice that most of the editorials touch only indirectly on the world of fashion. Rather they comment on a wide range of things—from climate change to population growth. It makes me wonder what I should write about for my first editorial. I lean back and stare at the door.

Then an idea flashes into my mind.

I'll write about an Englishwoman gazing at the Romans and their ways and describe how I react to what I see. With that settled, I decide to start on the piece right away. First develop an outline, then figure out the most important things to concentrate on.

Utterly lost in my thoughts, I'm unaware I'm not alone until someone clears his throat. My head jerks up. For a second it doesn't register then I jump up to my feet in confusion.

"Signore Ricci. I'm so honored to meet you," I say nervously.

He laughs, his face tight with plastic surgery. "I don't bite, you know."

"I'm sorry."

"Isn't that what the Americans say when they want to put you at ease?"

I smile with relief. "Yes, I suppose they do."

"Please, please, sit back down. I came to see how you like everything so far."

I remain standing, uncomfortable with the notion of sitting while he is on his feet. "Everything is …"

He strolls in. "A little overwhelming, yes?"

"Yes," I admit.

"That's why I'd like you to take some time to acquaint yourself with our beautiful city. I believe you know Rome only fleetingly."

"Yes, you're right."

"What do you think so far?"

My smile widens. "How could anyone not love Rome?"

"Splendid." He sits in one of the chairs and leans back, which allows me to slip into my chair too.

He regards me with clever, cunning eyes. "I'd like you to learn as much about the city as possible."

"I certainly hope to do just that."

"I'm going to make it a little easier for you to do so. Before you begin here, I'd like you to take at least a week off and become better acquainted with the city, our culture, the inhabitants."

I frown. "Before I begin work, Signore?"

"But of course. I would like you simply to learn and enjoy yourself while doing so."

I stare at him. "You want me to take time off to explore the city?"

"Definitely. You cannot write about what you do not know, nor can you write for people you do not understand. You'll need to know Rome intimately before you begin to write even one sentence."

"Yes, I see your point, Signore."

"Of course, you can come into the office whenever you wish

and confer with the staff. You are both a new resident and a new employee and have to adjust to both." He stands and walks toward the door. "We'll be seeing each other on occasion … though I generally like to take a 'hands off' approach." He salutes. "Arrivederci."

Surprise after surprise after surprise. This is going to be a wonderful job.

CHAPTER 14

Rosa

"*I* don't know, Star. I'm so confused. The sex is amazing. I mean, like really hot. And he's super charming as well, but if I keep going down this path I'm just going to get hurt. Bad."

"Why? Why do you always have to play it so safe? Just take a risk. You never know what could happen. I have a good feeling about him. I really liked him and I think you'll be good for each other. I can't explain it, but from the moment I met him I had a funny feeling that he was the one for you. That he was going to put a ring on it."

This is a funny conversation. It was usually me urging Star to take a risk and step out of her comfort zone. Then one day she took a leap out of it and has never looked back. "Yeah, he is fun, Star, but marriage material? Absolutely not," I say as I turn the covers back on my bed.

"You shouldn't be so hard on him, Rosa. Give him a chance. A baby can change a man."

I stop and sniff the air. "Oh my God, Star. I can smell cannabis wafting in through the windows. Must be the kitchen staff from the restaurant downstairs. I hope my baby doesn't inhale it."

Star giggles.

Suddenly, I hear an unfamiliar buzzing sound.

"And what the hell is that?" I mutter.

"What?' Star asks, her voice suddenly all concerned.

I glance around to see if there is an alarm clock I've missed. The buzzing comes again. "It's the downstairs doorbell!"

"Don't open the door, Rosa," Star whispers.

"I'll walk to the window and look down," I whisper back.

"Who is it?" she demands.

I sigh. "Who else but a playboy. See what I mean, Star. What am I now? A booty call?" With more than a hint of annoyance and the phone still in my hand, I hurry down the stairs. I unlock the door, and swing it open. The sharp words at the tip of my tongue die away.

"*Ciao, bella,*" Dante says standing with one arm propped against the side of the building. It's not fair. Damn him for looking like a model on the cover of *GQ*.

"Do you realize how late it is?" I ask, when I finally realize I should stop staring at him like a fool and say something.

"Of course I do. What better time to show you Rome than after dark when all the English tourists are in bed," Dante says, beaming his irresistible smile at me.

"Oh." I put the phone to my ear and hear Star laughing. I clear my throat.

"See what I mean?" she crows.

"I'll call you in the morning. Good night."

"Enjoy Rome," she sings before ringing off.

"Thanks for the thought, but I was actually about to go to bed."

His eyes widen thoughtfully, but to his credit he keeps his purpose. "Come on, let me take you out on a special excursion."

Hell, I want to cave in and go with him so much, it's embarrassing, but for my pride's sake I make a token protest. "But it's so late?"

He shakes his head. "I won't take no for an answer."

I make one last feeble attempt. "I'm already in my jammies."

"Didn't the owner of your magazine tell you to get acquainted with Rome before writing a single word?"

My eyes narrow. "Well yes, he did, but how do you know about that?"

"He told me, obviously."

I scowl and cross my hands over my chest. "Is he going to be giving you reports on me?"

"Don't be silly. Of course not. It was his first meeting with you and he happened to mention it."

"Right," I say suspiciously.

"Go on. Throw on a pair of jeans. I promise you won't regret it. If I am not the best tour guide in Rome, I don't know who is." He smiles, and the warmth of it melts the last bit of feeble resistance I have inside me.

"I suppose you better come in and wait while I change," I say hurrying back up the stairs.

I pull on a pair of white jeans and a lime-green crop top and go back out to the living room. He turns around from looking at my nest of photos. He walks over to me. Putting one finger under my chin he raises my face up to his. I stare into his eyes. They are almost yellow, like a wolf's.

"God, how could anyone look so fucking edible?" he mutters thickly.

I remember how he ate me out last night and blush like a teenager.

He smiles slowly. "I never thought I'd see you blush."

I open my mouth to say something cutting, but he lays his finger on my lips. "Sometimes, you don't need to say anything, *bella*."

Then he takes my hand and pulls me toward the stairs. "Come on. Rome awaits."

"Where's the taxi?" I ask, glancing around and expecting to see Salvatore parked nearby. When my eyes return to Dante, I find him taking helmets off a yellow Vespa.

"Oh, no. I'm not getting on the back of that thing with you!" I shake my head. "Those scooters are dangerous enough during the day."

"Rosa, where is your sense of adventure?"

"I'd have to say, back in London."

"Come on. All young lovers ride Vespas in Rome."

"Is that what we are?"

"Get on and find out," Dante says, holding out one of the helmets.

I hesitate for another second before I take it off him. "I hope I don't live to regret this," I mutter.

"You know Vespa means wasp in Italian," Dante adds sweetly as I climb on the back of the scooter.

"Yeah, I hope that name doesn't come from the sting you get

when you fall and hit the pavement!" I grumble, strapping on my helmet.

"Just hold me tightly and you won't fall," Dante advises, his eyes glinting.

I wrap my hands lightly around his hard body.

"Ready?"

"I think so," I answer, and he gives gas to the scooter causing it to lurch forward.

"Eeeeee!" I scream in terror as I tighten my grip around his waist.

"That's more like it," he says with an evil laugh.

"You did that on purpose, didn't you?" I accuse.

"Just relax," he calls over his shoulder.

I do more than just hold onto Dante's waist. I hug him so close my lips are pressing against the back of his neck as the wind blows into my face.

"Where are you taking me?" I shout to be heard over the noise of the scooter and the wind.

"It's a surprise," he yells back.

God, the streets are so different when viewing them while zipping around on the back of a Vespa. All of a sudden I realize that it doesn't matter where we're going. I'm enjoying both the ride and hugging Dante to ward off the fear I have of us crashing.

"We're here," Dante says pulling into the paved carpark of a fairly unremarkable restaurant/bar. It has a green awning and its name, *Lo Zodiaco* lit up. He turns off the ignition.

"You brought me to a restaurant?" I ask in surprise.

"I've brought you to the best kept secret in Rome. Go on, get down."

Pulling off my helmet, I get off the Vespa. He gets off too, and taking my hand leads me around the side of the restaurant.

"I give you Rome after dark," he says and points down at the city, ablaze in lights.

"Wow! Where *are* we?" I ask. The view of the city lights below is magical. I start walking forward towards the railing.

He joins me. "Monte Mario. This is the highest point in Rome."

"It's beautiful, Dante." I gaze spellbound at the majestic splendor of Rome spread out below me.

For a long while neither of us speaks then Dante puts his arm around me. "Lovers come here at night."

I turn my head and look at him. "Part of the seduction technique, is it?"

"One day that smart mouth of yours is going to earn you a good spanking, *Signorina*."

"Is that a promise?" I tease, knowing I'm completely safe.

"Getting cocky, are we?" Dante asks as he reaches out to grab my hand. I evade his hand and start running away from him. Catching me he whirls me around so I am inside the circle of his hands. My palms are on his chest and I can feel his heartbeat.

"I like it when you laugh," he says softly.

For a second my breath catches at the expression in his eyes, then I remember myself. I cannot let myself be swept up in his professional charm. "Where to now, Mr. Tour Guide?" I croak.

"You will soon see," Dante says, and leads me back to the Vespa. "All aboard for the last sight!"

"I'm sure it can't surpass this one." I climb up behind Dante.

"Ready?"

"As I'll ever be," I say, and then squeal like a schoolgirl when the Vespa lunges forward. "Do you bring all your lovers here?"

"No."

"Why not?"

"I never felt like it," he says simply.

"So why did you bring me?"

"Because I knew you'd enjoy it and I wanted to."

My belly feels warm. I turn my head to one side and press my cheek against his broad back. I feel like little Kai being taken by the Snow Queen in her sleigh. I feel enchanted.

Feeling the Vespa slow down, I raise my head. We have hit the narrow streets of downtown Rome.

"Oh, wow!" I exclaim as Dante stops the scooter.

"Fontana di Trevi, the largest fountain in Rome!" Dante announces as I climb off.

"It's golden! How beautiful! And it's so big!"

"The lights turn it gold at night. It's beautiful during the day, but at night it is very special. And no tourists!" Dante says sweeping his hands around.

"I love the winged horses."

"I like the statue of Poseidon most," Dante remarks.

"Being a macho man, you would."

I dig into my purse as I walk to the edge of the fountain. "I've got to toss a coin in," I say beaming.

"Be sure to close your eyes and make a wish."

I lean my upper body over the water, close my eyes, make a wish, and toss the coin into the air. When I hear it make a splash, I open my eyes.

Suddenly, Dante spins me around and presses his lips to mine. It feels as though an electric wire has touched my lips. As his tongue slips into my mouth, I swear I almost faint. He lifts his head and looks into my eyes. I can't look away. Then his powerful arms catch me as he bends his head and continues kissing me passionately.

I think of the Snow Queen kissing little Kai. Once to numb him from the cold, a second time to make him forget about Gerda and his family. I forget everything with that second kiss. It is the most romantic thing that has ever happened to me, and I know instinctively that as long as I live I'll never encounter such a kiss again.

Later, I surreptitiously kiss Dante's back as he drives us back to my house.

He waits for me to get off the scooter, takes my helmet, and buckles it on to the holder.

"Thank you, Dante. The night was enchanting, but especially the fountain."

And the kiss. God, the kiss.

"I would insist that you come up but I can barely hold my eyes open it's so late."

CHAPTER 15

Dante

https://www.youtube.com/watch?v=qpJ0cyXbMbI
Make me Smile (Come And See Me)

I stroke her soft cheek. This woman makes my dick rock hard and my insides melt.

Her lips tremble apart. "I guess you can come in for a quick coffee."

I smile. In my mind, she is already riding me, her warm pussy milking my cock, sucking every last drop of cum out of me. Her gaze stays locked on mine. I take the key from her fingers and slip it into the lock. Then I stand back and allow her to precede me. Her tight little ass trapped in her white jeans wriggles as she runs up the stairs. I catch her at the top. My cock is aching for her.

"The coffee," she whispers.

"Fuck the coffee," I growl.

There is not an ounce of fight in her when I sweep her into my arms and carry her into the bedroom. I lay her on the bed. Street light streams in from the window and falls on her cheek. Fuck, she is so damn beautiful. I'm going to do everything in my power to make her mine.

She stares up at me with wide eyes.

"Slide out of those jeans and show me your pretty cunt, Princess."

She gets up on her elbows. "Fuck you," she whispers back.

I grin. She likes it when I talk dirty but she just won't admit it.

"Go on. Show me what a dirty girl you are."

She kicks off her pumps and they fall to the floor with a soft thud, then she looks at me, a challenge in her eyes. I'll tame her, if it's the last thing I do.

I move my hand to the waistband of her jeans. She does nothing, but as I slide her zip down, her fingers reach out to grab me. I shake my head.

"It's all mine, *bella*," I tell her and her hands fall back to her sides. She watches me with those enormous, angel eyes, as I yank her jeans and panties down her legs and off her feet. I grab her ankles, open her legs, and look down at her wet cunt. I can see her little pussy pulsing with impatience, but I take my time. Slowly, I run my hands up her silky thighs and widen them so her whole pussy is completely exposed to my gaze.

"Fuck, you look so beautiful when you are spread open."

She inhales sharply, and I watch her thighs quiver with anticipation.

"Next time I ask you to show me your pretty cunt, you spread your legs real quick, because I'm going to see it and fuck it, anyway."

She wets her lower lips with her tongue. "So quit your talking and get on with it then."

Fuck, I love it when she's mad for me, but she tries not to show it. I place my palm on her dripping pussy and rub it gently. Her eyes glaze over and she moans softly. The wet heat from her pussy makes my cock swell to the point of pain.

I dip my finger into her sweet hole, and she groans and pushes up towards it.

I pull out of her.

"Don't stop," she begs. "Remember what you did that first night …" she bites her lip. "That's what I want again."

Hearing her ask for it makes me feel like a god. Her hands claw into my hair as I slip three fingers into her and suck her off. Her clit throbs in my mouth. Her scream of pleasure is wild and long, and she damn near pulls my hair out. As I unzip my pants I kiss her, forcing my tongue between her lips, so she can taste her own sweet pussy. I let her suck my tongue for a little while longer before I flip her around, and slam into her.

It's pure heaven.

She is hot and wet and tight as a virgin's ass. I've never fucked anyone else bare and it's amazing. From the time I was a teenager I knew I couldn't afford a mistake. An unplanned pregnancy. A disease. But she is just perfect. Perfect.

She raises her hips and bucks back against me, taking me even deeper into her body. She likes it rough and I give it to her rough. I want my cock to be the first thing she thinks of in the morning when she wakes up sore.

"Play with yourself," I grunt.

Her hand reaches under her body. "Oh fuck," she groans.

I watch my glistening shaft ram in and out of her until her pussy starts to clench. She comes hard on my cock. Watching her come makes me lose it. I hold her hips in place and empty every last drop of my cum inside her.

My climax lasts and lasts.

"I wish you could stay inside me all night long," she says softly.

I pull out of her and turn her around. Her eyelids are already half-closed.

"I was going to give you a blowjob," she whispers. "You like that, remember."

I shrug. "Nothing could make this night any better anyway. It was perfect." I lean forward and plant a kiss on her forehead. "Go to bed, Mommy. "I'll come by early tomorrow morning."

"Goodnight," she mumbles sleepily.

CHAPTER 16

Rosa

*S*omething warm and soft touches my lips and moves insistently against them. It feels so delicious as it gently wakes me from my sleep. I moan softly, the heavenly sensation goes away, and I reluctantly open my eyelids. A pair of whiskey eyes gaze down at me.

Sensuous lips curve upwards. Jesus, does the man have to be this sexy so early in the morning?

"You make me feel like the Prince who woke Sleeping Beauty," he drawls.

If there's one thing I don't feel like first thing in the morning, it's Sleeping Beauty. I rub my eyes. He went home last night. I heard the door close. I stop rubbing my eyes and stare at him. "Dante? How did you get in?"

"Since you haven't had the good sense to entrust me with a key, I had to ask your landlord, the owner of the pizzeria, to open your door."

My eyes pop open with surprise. "He did?"

"Of course. This is Italy, the land of passionate lovers. Only a smitten fool would come bearing coffee and *cannoli* this early in the morning."

I scowl. "He shouldn't have done that. You don't have a key because I don't want you to have a key. I'm not Italian. I'm English and we value our privacy."

Dante grins. "Good luck with convincing him."

"What's that supposed to mean?"

"You'll find out when you go have a pizza."

I think of pizza, all that melted cheese, and suddenly my stomach swirls.

"Now how about some breakfast?" Dante offers cheerfully.

I scrunch my face. "Oh, God. I feel sick. I think it must be morning sickness."

His eyes widen. "Charming. I bring you your breakfast in bed and you experience your first bout of morning sickness."

With a groan I push him away and dash toward the toilet. Thank heavens, I make it in time. I lean back against the tiles. Dante comes and crouches next to me.

"This is all your fault," I grumble.

"I'll go down the street and get something to make you feel better."

"Knowing my luck, I'm going to be nauseated for the rest of my pregnancy. Just see yourself out and leave me to my misery." I close my eyes.

He stands. "Be right back."

I make it to the bed feeling horrible. I lie back on the pillows and close my eyes. The sensation of wanting to throw up doesn't go away. I don't even open my eyes when I hear

Dante running up the steps, and feel my bed depress with his weight.

"Sit up and take a bite," Dante says.

I reluctantly open my eyes. Of course, he looks as fresh as a daisy. "What is it?"

He grins. "It's a magic potion."

"Uh huh, your magic potion looks a lot like stale biscuits." I observe as I take one from him and nibble at it. "Yuck, it tastes as old as Rome."

"Magic potions have to be old," Dante replies sagely. I can see he is making a great effort to keep from laughing. "Soon your stomach will settle."

"It doesn't feel like it will ever stop," I mutter as I take a second bite, and make a face.

"Oh, ye of little faith."

"Are you just going to sit here and watch me eat these biscuits?"

"Yeah," he says, folding his arms and making himself more comfortable.

I carry on nibbling the biscuit even though I can't imagine how it is going to help.

To my surprise though, half-way through my second biscuit I realize the queasy feeling is going away. "Hmmm."

"Yes?"

I brush the breadcrumbs still clinging to my lips and lean over to kiss Dante. "There might be a little bit of an old witch buried deep down inside of you, after all."

He shoots his cuffs and looks pleased with himself.

"How did you know to get those biscuits?" I ask curiously.

"I told you *Parenting Magazine.*"

"You were serious about that?" I ask, staring at him in surprise.

"I'm serious about our baby, Rosa."

I try not to show how confused I feel. It's true for most part I can't think straight around him, but what if …

"Get ready, *bella mia*. I'm taking you to the cemetery in Testaccio."

My jaw drops. "You are?" I told him while we were out at dinner that I loved walking through old cemeteries, but I never expected a Casanova who lives in a hotel suite to take me to one.

"Yes, I am," he says briskly. "A pregnant woman should never be denied anything her heart desires."

As hard as I try to dampen it, I can't help the flush of warm pleasure surging through my body. Hmmm … it is going to be very hard to resist him if he is going to be this nice and thoughtful. "Er … why don't you wait in the living room while I get ready?"

"You mean I can't stay and watch?" he asks incredulously.

I widen my eyes meaningfully.

"Probably best anyway. I'll just get turned on and you're obviously not in the mood," he says with a rueful shrug. Then adds hopefully, "Or are you?"

I shake my head in wonder. "Have you shake me around like a bottle of hot sauce when I feel this way? No thanks."

I watch him walk out of the bedroom with a little sigh. That's one sexy man-butt.

"*V*espa again?" I ask pretending to be disapproving, but secretly pleased.

"It's the best way to see the sights in this city, and it's perfect for parking." Dante hands me a helmet. "Although, it is a shame to hide that beautiful red hair of yours. I love to see it glow like a flame in the sunlight."

"You didn't by any chance stay up reading poetry?"

"Why do you ask?" Dante says, putting on his helmet.

"Your choice of words."

"Well, if one is going to visit Keats's grave, one must get in the mood."

I stare at him. "You know the location of John Keats grave?"

"Of course. As well as the grave of my favorite poet, Percy Bysshe Shelley."

"I should be surprised, but I've learned from watching *American Gigolo* that playboys must have a certain amount of culture."

He looks amused. "Isn't that movie about a male prostitute?"

"Frivolous playboy, male prostitute, what's the difference?" I say airily.

Dante gives the little scooter enough throttle to lift the front wheels clear off the pavement as we lurch forward suddenly.

I scream and he laughs.

"You do that again, Dante, and you'll be lying next to Percy Bysshe Shelley's bones!"

That makes him laugh even harder.

I try not to join him, but his laugh is infectious and it is impossible not to give in as we zip down the narrow streets on the Vespa. Before I realize it the side of my cheek is once again pressed against his back. Contentedly, I watch the buildings flash past in a blur of sun-warmed ancient stone.

Dante parks the Vespa under the leafy canopy of a large tree. "We walk from here."

As I climb off the back of the scooter, I glance around taking in the gnarled trees and the weathered gravestones nestled between shrubs and bushes. I beam at him. "What a great last resting place. Cemeteries make the most peaceful gardens."

"You weren't joking when you said you liked cemeteries, were you?"

"No, I wasn't. I love beautiful old graves. I don't know exactly why. Perhaps it is the wonder I feel that the nameless skeletons underneath were once flesh and bone like me. I guess it reminds me that time is short and I must leave my mark on the world in some manner, or another." I shrug. "Maybe a hundred years from now a stranger will visit my grave and say what a fantastic fashion editor I was," I joke.

Under the dappled shade of the tree we are standing Dante smiles indulgently, but his eyes are serious. "Actually, I bet lots of people will visit your grave."

I look at him curiously. "Why do you say that?"

"I'll tell you another time."

"Tell me now," I insist.

"Soon."

"Fine. Dante, the man of mystery."

"Come on," he says, taking my hand, and heading purposely down a path. We move from gravestone to gravestone stopping to read the inscriptions on the grander ones. "How surprising to see so many Russians and Englishmen buried here."

"It's a Protestant cemetery," he explains.

Quite close to the pyramid, Dante stops in front of a large rectangular gravestone with an arched top, and motions at it. "Keats." He says the name quietly with respect.

I move closer and read the inscription aloud. "'This grave contains all that was mortal, of a young English poet, who on his death bed, in the bitterness of his heart, at the malicious power of his enemies, desired these words to be engraven on his tombstone:

Here lies one whose name was writ in water.

*D*ante rubs my back. "Did I just see you shiver?"

I nod slowly. "I felt as if Keats had reached from beyond the grave and touched my soul." I look up at him. "Dante, why do you live in a hotel suite?"

He shrugs. "I move around a lot, and living in hotels mean I don't have to keep households full of staff everywhere I go."

I stare into his eyes. "Are you happy?"

"I thought I was." For a second something throbs between us. It could be the stillness of the cemetery, the strange expression on his face, or the way my heart thuds loudly against my ribcage, then the moment is gone when he grins and says, "Come, I have more graves to indulge your morbid tastes."

"Lead the way," I say, but as we walk away from Keats grave I can't help glancing back as though I'm leaving a precious moment behind.

"I'm getting hungry. How about you?" Dante asks.

My stomach rumbles. "Yes, but the thought of a real meal still makes me queasy."

"After we are done with the graves we'll go to the market and I'll buy some bread, olive oil, and balsamic vinegar for us. It will settle your stomach."

"Actually, that does sound very good," I surprise myself by saying.

I realize that we are back at the entrance and heading towards an area densely populated with headstones. "I present you the ashes of Percy Bysshe Shelley," Dante says gravely.

I walk closer to the plain headstone. "Percy Bysshe Shelley," I read out the name carved at the top of the headstone. I turn to face him. "How on earth does someone like you become a fan of Shelley?"

He laughs. "I wasn't until my uncle brought me a leather-bound collection of his complete works for my sixteenth birthday and told me he would buy me the latest sports car if I got through the collection. As you can imagine, I considered it a particularly vicious form of punishment, but by the second volume I had become a devoted fan."

"Are you from a very rich family?"

"Yes, I suppose I am."

"My Latin is rusty. What does 'Cor Cordium' mean?" I ask peering at the letters.

"Heart of hearts."

"What does that mean?"

"Legend has it that only his heart is buried here. While his body was being cremated on the beach, his friend, who lies in that grave next to him, snatched his heart out of the flames, and gave it to his wife who kept it for thirty years," Dante explains.

"That's a very romantic story." To my surprise, my eyes suddenly fill with tears for the man. "I don't know why, but ever since I got pregnant I seem to cry for the least thing," I sniff.

Dante takes my hand. "I love it when you are emotional. It is so rare for you to show your true self that these little outbursts are precious. Anyway, that is probably just a myth. What really happened is not so pretty. By the time Shelley's body was washed up it was so badly decomposed they could only identify him by his socks, trousers, and a volume of Keat's poetry in his pocket. The body was covered in quick-lime and temporarily buried in a shallow grave until permission for his cremation could be acquired. Mary did not attend the cremation. Byron was there, but became so nauseous he had to leave. If anything was snatched out of the ashes and given to Mary it was his liver which is the most moisture leaden organ in the human body and so least likely not to burn."

For a few seconds, I'm lost in his gorgeous eyes. "Deep down inside you are more than just eye-candy, aren't you?" I whisper.

Dante laughs. "Eye candy? Oh, Rosa, there is just no one else like you in the world."

I try not to show how pleased I am by that compliment. "Now, how about the bread with olive oil with balsamic vinegar you promised me."

CHAPTER 17

Rosa

*D*ante drives us to the market and we walk to a little food stand where he speaks in rapid-fire Italian to a middle-aged woman with braided hair and a blue apron. She wraps up a golden-brown loaf of bread and hands it to him.

We go to another stall where a wizened little man with a cheeky smile sells him a bottle of green extra-virgin olive oil and a plastic cup three-quarter filled with balsamic vinegar that his wife made.

We find a bench and tuck into our simple meal. The bread is crusty on the outside and open-textured on the inside, and absolutely delicious with the condiments. We don't talk much, both of us just content to enjoy the open air and each other's company. I pop the last piece into my mouth and wipe my hands on a paper napkin. "Thank you. That was really superb."

Dante squeezes my knee. "The pleasure was all mine, bella."

A little of me melts at that look in his eyes.

"Wait here while I throw this away," Dante says gathering all our leftovers in the paper bag the woman gave us.

I watch him stride away towards a bin. He is taller and broader than everyone else around him. I hear myself sigh. If only this man could be mine. Truly mine.

"Ciao, bella," a voice says from my side. I turn my head and a muscular, deeply tanned man in a tight white T-shirt is standing next to me. He lowers his sunglasses and smiles, showing very white teeth. His eyes are sly, though. I know what he wants from the tourist. From the corners of my eyes I can see Dante throw our rubbish away.

I smile at the guy. What I tell him makes his smile lose its luster. He turns and walks away just as Dante returns.

"Hey," I say, beaming at Dante. Just seeing the empty lust in the other man's face made me realize how sincere and full of care Dante's eyes are.

"What did that asshole want?" he asks, his jaw tight.

"I don't know. I didn't ask," I say.

He sits next to me, his back rigid.

"What's the matter with you?"

"Nothing."

I stare at his closed profile incredulously. "Are you jealous?"

He turns to look at me and his eyes are blazing. "Of course I am. I'm a man. I know what goes through men's heads. You should never flirt with opportunists."

"I was not flirting with him."

"Encouraging him, then," he says, his eyebrows meeting.

"Encouraging him?" I gasp, suddenly furious too. "Where did you see that?"

"You were smiling at him."

I take a deep breath. "Okay, I am willing to admit that from a distance it could look like I was smiling, but actually it was the curve of my mouth as I told him, *'Vatte a fa' 'u giro, a fessa 'e mammata.'*"

His eyes widen. Then he scratches his head. "Do you … er … know the meaning of what you just said?"

"Yes. I told him in perfect idiomatic Italian to piss off back up the orifice of his mother's vagina."

"That's my girl. You tell every one of those shit bags who have the nerve to come up to you exactly that, in exactly that same tone."

I smile up at him. "Okay."

He nods and ruffles my hair the way a proud father would.

"So what now? Home?"

"No, unless you are tired, of course."

"Nope. Not tired at all."

"Then I have another creepy place to show you."

"What is it?"

"You will see soon enough."

"Today you are full of surprises, Dante, and so far, all of them were good so lead on." I strap on the simple open-faced helmet and climb onto the back of the bright yellow Vespa.

I hate to admit it, but I don't think I will ever get tired of zipping around Rome on the back of Dante's scooter.

*D*ante whirls his hand like a ringmaster at a circus and points at a building with double stairs. "You wanted morbid, I give you morbid. Behold the Capuchin

Crypt of the Church of Santa Maria Della Concezione," he declares dramatically.

I look at the unremarkable brown chapel in front of us and am not impressed.

"You judge too quickly, *bella*. Churches and men," Dante says softly. "Wait until you discover what's inside before you make up your mind."

"Okay, but I wasn't making a judgment, just noting a totally warranted observation about the exterior," I say.

"Exteriors can be very deceiving," he says as we enter the chapel. I know he is not referring to the building, but my opinion of him.

I scan the interior of the church and my eyes light up as I spot the tall stunning painting of the archangel Michael. "Okay, now we are talking. That is quite simply marvelous," I exclaim, squeezing Dante's hand.

"That it is, but I didn't bring you here to show you Guido Reni's painting," Dante says. "Come, follow me into the crypt."

"Ooooouuuu, that sounds spooky," I say smiling as I follow him down into the bowels of the church. It is kind of eerie walking into the dark and very ancient chamber.

"Close your eyes," Dante tells me when we reach the bottom of the stairs. "I'll tell you when you can open them," he adds taking my hand again.

"Don't you dare let me fall. There's a baby on board."

"I will never let you fall," he whispers in my ear, and his voice startles me with its intensity. I open my eyes and stare into his. For a second it feels as if the air is too ancient and thick and it is impossible to breathe it in, then Dante says, "Close your eyes, little Rosa."

I obey, and feel him take my hand and lead me farther into

the crypt. We must have been somewhere near the center of the room when he says. "Okay, you can look now."

I open my eyes and see … bones; hundreds, maybe even thousands of bones. Bones nailed into every inch of wall and ceiling, hanging from the ceiling as light fixtures, just piled into heaps, or used as baroque decorative details. There are skeletons dressed as monks. The display is at once, intricate and fantastic.

"Are … Are they all real?"

"Every single bone and skull you see belonged to one of the three thousand seven hundred dead Capuchin monks who were used to decorate these crypts," Dante explains.

"Were they captured prisoners?"

"No, all of them were monks themselves."

"Whoa, they used their own dead brethren. That is even more fascinating."

He looks at me curiously. "So you like it?"

"I probably should be horrified by all these dead men's bones, but I'm not. It's actually pretty amazing how they turned something that most people consider gruesome into décor. I mean, look at that archway made of human skulls!" I exclaim as my eyes explore the room further. "And those. They're spinal bones, aren't they? Wow! Check out those leg bones making a pirate cross over the doors," I say, turning in a circle. "I have never, never seen anything like this in my life, Dante."

One by one we explore the other crypts. Each crypt is made with a body part. There is a crypt of shin and thigh bones, a crypt of pelvises, and a crypt of skulls.

"Do you know that cappuccino is named after the color of the Capuchin monks robes?" Dante murmurs.

"Really?" I say, filing away the information to use in an article.

The last chamber is adorned with the full skeletons of two Barberini princelings. Near them is a placard that drives home the point of the entire display. The message is printed in several languages.

What you are, we used to be.
What we are, you will become.

CHAPTER 18

Rosa

"*H*ow is your stomach now?" Dante asks as we finally walk out of the church.

"Strangely enough, it feels almost normal."

"Then I have a treat for you," Dante says.

He takes me to a small café on a nearby street with tables on the sidewalk.

"I trust you completely after today, Dante."

Dante choses a table under a small shady tree and holds the chair out for me.

"Thank you," I say with a big smile as I take my seat.

Almost immediately a waiter with white hair and a stare that seems to say he has seen and heard it all, approaches our table. He has a white towel draped over his forearm. He glances at me and nods politely. "*Signorina.*"

"As always," Dante tells him in Italian.

He nods politely and goes away.

"And what did you order?"

"*Carciofi alla Guida*, Jewish style artichokes."

"What in heaven's name are Jewish style artichokes?"

"Fried artichokes."

I look at him doubtfully. "I'm not a fan of artichokes at the best of times, but with being pregnant I could throw up in your lap. I hope you're not going to make me regret trusting you."

He looks at me confidently. "I'm not worried. I'll be very surprised if you don't love them."

The waiter brings us a large bottle of ice cold water and two glasses.

He starts to say something else but the old waiter appears beside the table and places our plates in front of us.

I pick up a crispy golden morsel, pop it into my mouth, and savor the lemony taste on my tongue before chewing it. "It's actually delicious. Consider me officially impressed."

"Yes, I thought you would enjoy the dish," Dante says smugly.

Ignoring him I begin to devour my food.

"You have a good appetite," Dante notes with some astonishment.

"Eating for two," I mumble while stuffing my face. "God, I hate to think how fat I'm going to get."

"You will only grow more beautiful," Dante says softly.

"Ah, the silver-tongued playboy fights his way to the surface again."

He puts his fork down, his eyes narrow. "I was being honest. You will benefit with a few extra pounds."

"Oh yeah? Don't tell me, I will also benefit from some stretch marks."

He shrugs. "What's wrong with a few stretch marks?"

"You say that, but have you ever slept with a girl with stretch marks before?"

His eyes glitter with something that looks almost like anger. "Does it matter what I did in the past? People can change, Rosa. You have judged me and you hardly know me."

The air between us becomes heavy. I so much want to believe him. "Then tell me about Dante," I say softly.

"Tomorrow, I will tell you everything."

"Why not now?"

"Because you're tired and it's a long story."

"Swear it."

He grins. "I swear upon my sword."

"Hmmm, a metal one or the one between your legs?" I astonish myself by saying.

"I'll let you know when we get back to your apartment," Dante shoots back, a wicked look in his eyes as his hand lifts for the bill.

Just like that all the fears that I have no future with him retreat to a far corner of my mind and all I want to do is make mad, crazy love to him.

I cheat on the ride home. Instead of wrapping my arms around his waist, I reach down and grab his cock as we zip along on the Vespa. At least, I start out just holding his growing shaft, but long before we reach the pizzeria I am rubbing the crotch of his pants as though it were a bottle with a genie inside. The long and thick genie inside his pants is full-grown by the time Dante parks the Vespa in front of the pizza shop.

When he gets off the scooter the front of his slacks is in the shape of a tent.

"Wow," I whisper, my eyes glued to the big bulge in his pants.

"You did that, Princess, you made me as horny as fuck."

I lick my lips and he snatches my wrist. "That's right, baby, you need to get on your knees and get that sweet tongue on my dick real quick."

I hurry behind him. I can't wait to get him in my mouth. To taste him. To make him lose control. He pulls me towards my door. I pull my key out of my purse. My fingers feel like butter as I fumble with the lock and drop the key.

Dante puts his hand briefly over mine before reaching down and picking up the key. "Let me."

The lock yields instantly to Dante's hand. No doubt he has lots of experience opening women's doors in moments of excitement, I can't help thinking, but I don't say anything.

CHAPTER 19

Rosa
https://www.youtube.com/watch?v=-Oo_73SlOwk
A quiet angel on the sun
UnAngelo Disteso Al Sole

*H*e pushes me inside, kicks the door shut, and slams me against a wall as our lips meld. I close my eyes and he presses his hard body against mine. I can feel his cock, hot and hard digging into me.

Breathlessly, I allow his tongue to probe, sweep, and caress. Pleasure jolts all the way down to my toes. Desire such as I have never felt before makes me drop to my knees and reach out for his beautiful cock. I don't care that I am suddenly acting like a slut. I want his cock. I want to taste it, to devour it. I moan as my fingers touch his soft, warm skin.

He pulls away from me, takes his cock out and holds it out to me. To my shock I realize that his hands are shaking with raw need.

I can feel his eyes on me, wild and hungry. "Open up, Princess," he groans thickly.

I slide my fingers down the shaft of his long thick cock and grab hold of it at the base. Still looking up, I eagerly lick the tip, glistening with a bead of pre-cum. It maddens him, and makes his hands claw into my hair. I open my mouth wide and slip my lips over the big head of his cock.

As I close my eyes to savor the taste of him, Dante inhales sharply and tenses.

"Fuck," he groans as I suck him to the back of my throat. I want to take all of him into my mouth, but I have to be content with just over halfway. I bring my hands up and stroke the length of cock that I can't get into my mouth, rubbing the satin skin. I lick the underside of his shaft and he groans again.

"Jesus, baby, you feel so fucking amazing."

I feel his excitement and it makes me almost dizzy to think of how much he wants this. His cock throbs in my mouth as I suck him harder and deeper. Holding onto my head he starts to pump in and out. I feel spit running down my chin when he fucks my mouth, but I don't care. I kneel there and take it. All of a sudden I am so turned on I slip my hand down my skirt. His eyes widen with interest.

"I want to watch," he growls.

I hike my skirt up to my waist and tuck it into my waistband. Then I widen my thighs and let him watch me push aside the material of my panties and touch my pussy. I see that he can hardly hold on as I start swirling my fingers around my clit. My hand speeds up as his thrusts become more and more urgent. When I least expect it, he pulls his cock out of my mouth.

"Fuck it, I got to eat your pussy. I want to sixty-nine with you, taste your orgasm and watch you swallow my cum."

He gets on the floor and pulls me on top of him. His strong hands curl around my ribs. As if I'm nothing more than a doll, he spins me so my head is facing his feet. He tears my panties and spreads my legs open.

As I slip my lips over his erect cock, I feel his mouth greedily latch on to my pussy. He is first to go over. He swirls his tongue around my clit as he empties his hot seed into my mouth. I swallow every last drop and keep on sucking even as he pulls my orgasm from me. I come in a great rush, gushing into his mouth. He cleans me up with his tongue.

"I want to taste another orgasm," he says.

When I wriggle in protest, he spanks my ass and tells me, "I can do whatever I want with this body. It belongs to me now."

In that position and with his dick slowly hardening again inside the warm cave of my mouth, he gives me two more orgasms, before he says, "That's enough for now. I want to come inside my dirty girl."

He pulls me upright and turns me to face him. Holding me by my hips he positions the entrance of my swollen pussy over the saliva dripping head of his cock. Then he cups his hands on either side of my face down and kisses me, thrusting his tongue into my mouth so I taste my own juices. Still kissing me passionately, he enters me with a wild thrust of his hips.

I cry out in a mixture of pleasure and pain as he rams his cock deep inside of me. I feel like a virgin getting fucked for the first time. His cock is so long and thick it always feels like he is shoving a spear into me.

As I get used to how deep he is I start to take pleasure in being so stretched, so filled. I moan softly as his hips begin to slowly thrust forward. Slowly, his deliciously slow grinding rhythm turns into a quick pumping action.

"You are mine," he roars so loudly, I'm sure the customers

eating pizza down below must have heard his proclamation of ownership.

"Yes, yes, yes," I cry out as I feel his cream gushing into me. The sensation triggers an orgasm and suddenly I am hunching his cock as he cums inside of me. I can't stop moving my pussy up and down, up and down.

When I go limp with exhaustion, I feel Dante's strong arms come up to support me. Somehow, I am on the floor and he is lifting me. I open my eyes as he carries me into the bedroom. He lays me gently onto the bed.

"Sleep, my beauty. Tomorrow, I will take you for lunch and we will talk," he says, he bends down and kisses me on the forehead.

I want to ask him to spend the night, but I'm suddenly so incredibly tired. Ever since I became pregnant my exhaustion is all encompassing. I can hardly manage to nod my head as lethargy overtakes me. I am vaguely aware of him turning and walking out of the bedroom.

Then sleep descends over me like a black curtain.

CHAPTER 20

Dante

https://www.youtube.com/watch?v=0RyInjfgNc4
Love On The Brain

I walk to the door and even open it. I pause for a moment, then I close it and go back to her bedroom. Just one more last look at her.

She is already fast asleep.

Her skin and hair glow in the soft moonlight slanting in through the window. Her beauty makes her seem like an angel. The hairs at the back of my neck lift and I feel an almost divine electric current run through my body. What the fuck? An instant longing rises in me, a mix of lust and possessive need for her.

As if I have never fucked her, all I want to do is fucking worship her pussy.

I want to see her naked again.

To bare my soul to her.

My cock is so hard, my hands clench at my sides. Hell, I desperately want to touch her, to crush her to my chest, smooth her hair, and kiss away her fears. But I will not wake her up. She needs the sleep. She is with child now. My child. The thought worries me. She seems too fragile to carry a baby to full term.

I can still smell our coupling. It lingers on her skin. I bend down and lightly touch her skin, but she is so deeply asleep she does not even stir. I kiss her parted mouth gently. She moans and moves towards me. Sexual energy awakens like a snake in me. My cock swells painfully and I feel my body vibrate with desire. If I stay here any longer I'm going to end up between her legs again. With a frustrated groan, I turn around and walk away.

I close her front door softly and go down the street. From inside the pizzeria, Antonio, the owner, calls to me. The place is busy and his waiters are busy, but he is sitting at his usual table. I go in and he orders two glasses of grappa for us. He sweeps back his wiry, white hair and smiles broadly.

"How does it go?" he asks in Italian.

"Good," I say with a smile.

We down the ice-cold grappa and he invites me to join him for supper. "Liver marinated in fish sauce and grilled over an open fire."

Antonio is an interesting guy. He owns five of these restaurants, but he has stories from when he worked as a laborer in Germany. Funny stories of visiting German brothels, and eating shoe leather when he was really broke, but tonight I'm not in the mood for company, or Roman offal no matter how beautifully done.

I am restless and agitated.

Tonight my mind and body are buzzing like never before.

I decline his generous offer, and bidding him goodnight I leave the restaurant. I get on the scooter and long for the feel of her body behind me. The streets are full of lovers strolling. They live their lives lightly. They never think of this city's rich, dark, pungent, blood-soaked history. I never forget it. Their laughter as I pass them by touches my skin. I never told her. Her laugh gives me goosebumps. It is sexy as fuck.

I get back to the hotel and go up to my suite. I pour myself a large drink. I wanted so bad to stay with her tonight. I've never wanted to stay with any woman beyond the exchange of pleasure, but this woman lures me like a siren. I never want to leave her company. She feels right. She fits into me like two pieces of a jigsaw puzzle. As if she is a part of me.

I throw myself on to my bed and close my eyes.

I can still smell her sex, its unique scent clings to me as if it were a perfume. I fill my nostrils and visualize her again, her pale soft body, naked and willing, surrendering to my every need as I fill her with my tongue, my fingers, my cock.

The craving for her is strong; I want to go back outside, jump on the Vespa and go straight to her place. I want to rush up those rickety stairs, pull her from the bed, and fuck her in every room, across the furniture, against the wall, all night long until we are both so spent from exhaustion we sleep where we fall.

But not tonight.

I will be patient. I will wait.

Tomorrow I will tell her everything.

CHAPTER 21

Rosa

*T*hough I hadn't fancied the thought of getting on a Vespa the first time, I now look forward to it. I've grown to love the feel of fresh air blowing against my body and the sensation of being a part of the environment rather than just an observer enclosed inside a metal box. Okay, I admit, it's also an extremely erotic thing to be nestled close to Dante's hard, muscular body and feel the sure confidence flowing from it.

In anticipation of the ride in the wind I'd dressed in cream Capri pants, a lavender jersey top, and sensible pumps. The jersey top is a bit risqué, since it's tight and low cut, but I figure I better wear this sort of thing now before my belly gets too big.

The doorbell rings at five minutes to 1.00 p.m.

Grabbing my purse, I run lightly down the stairs and open the door. Dante is in a beautifully cut dove-grey suit with a black shirt open two buttons down. His hair falls adorably over his forehead.

"How do you feel?" he asks with a captivating smile.

My heart actually skips a beat. I hold up my crossed fingers. "So far so good."

His eyebrows rise. "No more morning sickness?"

"Yes, but I ate the rest of your magic biscuits and they worked a treat."

He flashes another megawatt smile. "I'm glad. I'll get you some more later."

"Where's the scooter?" I ask looking around.

Laughing he steps forward and brushes his lips lightly with mine. "I thought we'd try a different mode of transportation today, and maybe from now on." He takes my hand and draws me to his side facing the street. "M'lady," he says in a fake English accent, "your chariot awaits."

The chariot is a shiny red Ferrari. Talk about playboy clichés. "Wow! It's obviously not the one your uncle gave you for reading Shelley."

Dante laughs. "No, this one is a 488GT. 570-horsepower and probably the best V8 ever produced. It's a hell of a lot faster than the one my uncle gave me, but it's kind of wasted on the streets of Rome."

"It's a supercar."

"I'm glad you approve." He takes my arm, leads me to the door, and opens it.

I hesitate. "Dante?"

"Yes."

"Are we going somewhere really fancy?" I look down at my clothes. "I thought we doing cemeteries and crypts. I can go back upstairs and change."

His eyes flash with something fierce and possessive. It makes them look like liquid gold. "There's not a place in this world you couldn't go just as you are," he says. "Now get in before I change my mind and take you upstairs to show you just how fucking edible you look."

With a happy smile I quietly slip into the seat. When he closes the door and goes around the back to the driver's side, I reach down and touch the exquisite tan-colored, leather seat. It is as soft as butter.

Dante gets in beside me, making the space feel very small.

"Ready?"

"Uh … huh," I reply, and instantly the powerful engine roars to life. It's a throbbing sound that fills me with excitement.

Dante steps on the gas pedal, and all of a sudden the red car is screeching at breakneck speed down the narrow streets of Rome.

"Dante! Dante, slow down!" I shout in a panic, but he puts his hand on my leg and says, "Rosa, Ferraris are meant to be driven fast. Relax and enjoy the ride."

After that he continues to zip in and out of traffic as though we're in a chase scene from a *Fast and Furious* movie. Gripping my purse tightly, I watch him barely miss colliding with other motorists who to my surprise, seem utterly unfazed by his erratic driving. One or two even take time to gaze approvingly at Dante's car.

"Where are we going?" I ask trying to distract myself from the fact that we must be going at what feels like 200 kilometers per hour.

Dante glances at me. "It's a surprise."

By the time the white knuckle ride comes to a neck-snapping stop in front of a restaurant, I'm almost ready to make the sign of the cross.

"Here we are," he announces.

I look at the unobtrusive front. "Hmmm … a restaurant called Luigi's."

"Remember what I told you about judging the book by the cover."

"I'm not judging," I defend. "Merely making another valid observation."

He touches my nose with his finger. "Well, *bella mia*, let me tell you, the other Luigi's can't even begin to compare with this one."

A young man dressed in black approaches. "May I, sir?" he asks in Italian.

Dante slips out of the car, hands him the car key, and comes around to my side. Laying his hand on the small of my back, he leads me towards the glass entrance.

"By the way," I say quietly, "if you plan to drive home the way you drove here, kindly call me a taxi."

Dante laughs. "You'll get used to my driving."

He holds the door while I enter. A young woman sitting behind a desk nods at Dante. A man in a suit opens an inner door, and the interior of the restaurant nearly takes my breath away. No cheap, checkered tablecloths, or dripping candles stuck in Frascati bottles either. Rather, the décor is elegant and understated with dark leather and wood—the way a British gentlemen's club might look. The air is cool and hushed. There are customers eating, but they are screened by potted palms. I gaze at the fine oil paintings decorating the walls.

"Told you this place is different from any other Luigi's," Dante murmurs in my ear.

A maître d' approaches us with a welcoming smile and shows us to our table. The whitest of cloths covers it, and monogrammed white linen napkins rest by each place.

"Do you trust me to order?" Dante asks.

"Sure," I murmur, a little overwhelmed by my surroundings.

A waiter approaches with two menus, which Dante waves away, and beckons him to come closer instead. He inclines his head toward Dante, and the two confer for a minute or two. Dante calls the man Guissepe, and he in turn addresses him as Signore Dante.

"I'm starting to believe that you know the names of all the waiters in Rome," I say once Guissepe leaves the table.

His eyes crinkle at the corners with amusement. "But, of course. Isn't that part of a playboy's job—to get everyone on his side."

"They all know you because you are such a big spender?"

His smile broadens. "That would be a safe assumption to make."

I nod. "So what did you order?"

"For the first course we are having a variation of *Cacio e pepper.*"

"I've never had it. What is it?"

"Pecorino Romano cheese and fresh black pepper pasta are swirled with cooking water from the pasta to make a creamy sauce. Then pasta, smoked pork jowl, and egg are added. It is an extremely simple and light dish, but superb when well done. They do it perfectly here. Our second course is oxtail slow-cooked with San Marzano tomatoes in a stew until the meat is so tender it falls right off the bone."

"You're making my mouth water."

At that moment Guiseppe arrives with the wine. Respectfully, he shows the label to Dante, who approves with a slight nod. He begins to pour a glass for me. "Not for me—," I say.

"Yes, you will have one mouthful today," Dante interrupts. "This is very good wine and we are toasting to our first born."

I stare into his eyes. *Firstborn: the first of many.* His eyes are veiled and watchful. The thought of being part of a family with him makes my head swim.

He raises his glass. "To our baby."

"To the baby," I echo faintly before taking a sip. The wine is cool and delicious on my tongue. I watch him over the rim of my glass. It still feels strange to think that I'm carrying his baby. That this man I thought I would never see again, is the father of my child. He puts his wine glass down. There is an unusually serious look on his face.

"What is it?" I ask.

"I have a confession to make."

CHAPTER 22

Rosa

"*W*hat about?" I try to keep my tone neutral, but it comes out wary.

"First of all, I'm not Italian."

My eyes widen. "You're not?"

He shrugs. "I'm not. I was neither born here, nor am I a citizen."

"Okay," I say slowly. "So where are you from?"

"I am from the kingdom of Avanti."

Of course, I'd learned about that tiny landlocked tax haven in my Geography lessons, but until now I had never actually met anyone from there. I look at him curiously. "So why pretend to be Italian?"

He holds up a hand. "For the record, I never actually said I was Italian. You assumed I was and I didn't correct you."

"Why?"

He shows the first sign of discomfort. "I'm getting there, Rosa. What I really want to tell you is that my full name is not Dante D'Angelo but Nils Dante de Beauvouli."

The world stops spinning. There is only him and me suddenly. "De-Beauvouli?" I repeat in shock.

"Precisely."

"As in ..."

He nods. "King Isak Elliot De-Bouvouli is my father."

"What?" My hands flail. I can't believe what he's saying. "You're a prince?"

"I am."

"But you can't be ..."

His mouth quirks. "Because I'm only a playboy?"

"Yes. I mean, no. Oh, my God, I'm sorry I said all those things."

"Calling me a playboy? Thinking I can't settle down."

I cover my cheeks with my palms. "It explains all the things you know. The poetry and ... but I work for fashion magazines. I should know about you. Why are the paparazzi not all over you?"

"Because I walked away from it all before I was eighteen. My father put a news blackout on me. No one talks about me. I'm just another playboy."

My jaw drops. "You walked away from being a prince? Why would anyone do *that*?"

"Because I don't believe that it should be anyone's birthright to rule a country. One has to deserve the power to rule. It should be based on consensus and merit."

"So who will take over after your father?"

"I have a younger half-brother, but our tradition states that succession must now skip to the next generation."

I stare at him in wonder. "Does your brother have children?"

He shakes his head.

I gasp. "You mean our child will be the next King or Queen of your country."

"Yes," he says simply.

I fan my face with my hands. "Oh my God!"

"Rosa ..."

"Yes?" I whisper.

He reaches into the side pocket of his jacket and pulls out a velvet box. He opens it and I nearly faint. Inside is the most beautiful rectangular blue stone I have ever seen.

"Dante." I feel myself blushing. "I shouldn't even be calling you that anymore, should I?"

"What do you mean?"

"You're Prince Nils!"

He throws his head back and laughs. "I'm the same caveman who ate you out last night."

"Why don't you say that louder. I'm sure they didn't hear it in the kitchen," I hiss.

"I'll scream it from the rooftops if you want."

I ignore his comment and lay my hands against my temple. All this is just too much for me to process. "But surely you can't just marry a commoner?"

"I can marry anyone I want."

"But Royals don't marry commoners."

"Marrying other royals helped to consolidate power in the past, and today it helps to maintain the illusion of a blood-line's purity. I don't subscribe to the notion that just blood-line alone makes someone special, so, Rosa Winchester, will you marry me?"

Suddenly, I'm so tense I can hardly breathe.

"For the sake of our baby," he adds, "I know you've doubted my sincerity about wanting to be part of my child's life, but I want to be a real father to him or her. It's very important to me." He stops and looks into my eyes. "I'll be the first to admit I was not ready to settle down, but most of it was a pretence. I was lying to myself. Pretending my life was perfect. And from the outside it was. A hedonistic life, a non-stop party. From one country to another the goal was simply pleasure, but a part of me was never satisfied. In the end all those bodies, all those hot nights, all those fun parties become meaningless. I don't miss any of it. Right now, there's an important party on a yacht in Monte Carlo, but there is not even one cell in my body that wishes I was anywhere else, but here with you."

"I ..."

"We could make a great life together."

"I'm sure we could, but—"

"There are no buts. Life is what we make it."

"It's just ... it's such a shock. I mean, I feel like pinching myself to make sure I'm not dreaming. I thought it was too good to be true when I was offered the job at the magazine here, but this! This definitely can't be real. You're a prince and I'm carrying a royal baby inside me! It's too unbelievable. It's almost like a fairytale."

He makes a face. "Trust me, it's hardly a fairytale. Of course, we have our traditions, but for all the pomp and circum-stance we have to go to the toilet like everybody else."

"Go to the toilet," I repeat stupidly.

He grins. "'Fraid so."

I can't help myself. I laugh almost hysterically. "It's just that when a person thinks of a king and queen, it's never imagining them sitting on a toilet."

"You have something against toilets, do you?"

Suddenly, I start to laugh and can't stop.

He joins in the laughter. "I'm going to have to convince you, Rosa, that we're just human beings." His eyes are suddenly serious. "I want you and my baby in my life."

My heart pounds like a drum. Confused, I grab his glass of wine and take a big mouthful, then suddenly remember my baby, and look around me in a panic.

"Spit it back into the glass," Dante advises calmly.

Doing as he suggests, I dab my lips with the napkin. To my horror, a waiter comes by and discreetly removes the glass. Heat rushes up my throat, but I clear it, and look up into Dante's watching eyes.

"So what do you say?" he asks.

"What about my job?"

"We can live here. Nothing needs to change. The only thing we will be doing is giving our baby two parents who love it and place its interest above all else."

When he puts it that way, what can I say? "Let me think for a minute, will you please?"

His lips stretch. "Of course. Take all the time you need."

"Thank you. I need to think this through." My mind whirls. Dante and I get along extremely well and enjoy each other's company, in fact, I can't think of anybody else I would rather spend time with, and of course, the sex is amazing. But we don't love each other so it will be a sort of sham marriage. On the other hand, the baby deserves to have both a mother and a father. Also it wouldn't be fair to deprive the child of its rightful standing. My child is going to be the King of a kingdom one day. I'm going to be queen mother!

Whoa!

Never in all my life, even as a little girl, have I ever pretended to be a princess or a queen. I always wanted to be the kickass heroine who saves the day with clever thinking and fast action. What do I know about being royalty? Nothing.

"Your minute is up," Dante says.

I look at him. His eyes are laughing and he is so beautiful I want to do him right there. As if a switch gets turned inside my head, I come to a sudden decision. "All right. I accept."

His eyebrows fly up and his joy is genuine. "That's wonderful. You won't regret it, *bella*. You will see for yourself that we are just ordinary people who sit around watching TV and drinking beer."

"Except your mum and dad wear crowns."

His eyes twinkle. "Almost never. And you want to know something else?"

"What's that?"

"My crown is stuck away in a dark closet somewhere in the palace and surrounded by moth balls."

"Moth balls!"

"I'm kidding, Rosa. I have never worn a crown, and never will." He's quiet for a moment. "Speaking of meeting my family ..." He leans forward and kisses me lightly on the lips. "I've told my father and stepmother about you."

I stare at him in shock. "You've already told them about me?"

Unfazed he beams back at me. "Right after you moved to Rome."

"What did you tell them?"

"I told them I'd met the woman I wanted to marry."

"Did you tell them about the baby?"

"Of course. They want to meet you."

"They want to meet me?" I echo blankly.

"Yes. There's a ball this weekend and the king would love to have you attend."

"A ball? This weekend?" I'm so flustered I can barely think. "I … er … I have nothing suitable to wear. You know, nothing has arrived yet from London. And … even if it had … I hardly think I have anything that is suitable for a royal ball."

I stop babbling when Dante's large, tanned hand covers mine. "You worry too much, *bella*."

"Maybe we can meet him another time."

"No. There is no point putting it off. We will go this weekend."

"Why is it important that your father meet me this weekend?"

"He would like to introduce you."

"Introduce me?" I repeat.

"As my future wife?"

My eyes pop open. "You told them we were going to be married?"

"I didn't plan on taking no for an answer."

"Dante, everything's moving too fast. I can't keep up."

"It'll be all right. Believe me." He reaches for my hand. "Let's see how good a fit this is." He takes my hand and places the ring on my finger. It's a perfect fit.

I'm marrying a prince! I can't believe it. I'm really marrying a prince. I'm living every girl's dream!

As if on cue waiters arrive bearing food. They place the plates in front of us and fuss around us with pepper grinders and parmesan graters.

"Bon appétit," Dante says when they are gone.

Automatically I pick up my fork and slip a piece of pasta into my mouth. I'm in such a state of shock I don't taste anything.

"What do you think?" Dante asks.

"Pure heaven," I lie.

CHAPTER 23

Rosa

"*H*ello," Star says.

I'm about to speak, but as I hold my hand up the overhead light in my kitchen catches the huge blue diamond and makes it reflect hundreds of pieces of sparkling blue light all over the ceiling.

"Rosa?" Star prompts.

"Dante is a prince, and he asked me to marry him," I blurt out.

"What?"

"Dante is a prince, and he asked me to marry him!"

She giggles. "Have you been drinking at lunch?"

"No, I haven't. He's a real prince, Star. His father is the King of Avanti."

For a few seconds Star goes completely silent. "Are you serious?" she asks finally.

"Absolutely."

"Dante is a prince?" she squeals.

"Yes," I confirm, my voice matching her excited squeal.

"For real?"

"Yes."

"Nooooooo," she screams.

"Star, there is a blue diamond ring on my finger that is as big as that spider we found in your shoe cupboard!"

Star screams again, so loudly this time she nearly deafens me! "Oh my God! Oh my God!" she shouts into the phone, then screams again. "I can't believe this. You are going to be a princess! Oh, my God. I'm going to faint. Let me sit down. I feel quite lightheaded. I swear, I'm going to faint."

"Star, you are more excited than I am! Well, not really, but almost."

"This is so exciting. Okay. I'm sitting. Now tell me everything."

"You know we were having lunch today, right?"

"Yes."

"Well, he came to pick me up in this bright red Ferrari. The leather seats were so soft I just kept fondling it."

"Can you please get on with your story?"

"Then he took off like a bat in hell, and I was gripping my purse in mortal fear. You should see the way he drives."

"Rosa, just skip to the part where he told you he is a prince, please."

"Right. During lunch. He opened the conversation by saying he had a confession to make." Then I proceed to tell her about the royal family of De-Beauvouli about the fact that our baby will be the heir to the throne since Dante has relinquished his claim to the throne."

"Wow!" Star breathes. "Why did he relinquish his claim?"

"He doesn't believe in it, apparently."

"Wow."

"I know."

"You sound so calm. Do you see how big this is? Your baby will be a King! Or a Queen."

"I wasn't this calm a few hours ago."

"I bet you never screamed or cried."

"That's true. I didn't do either of those things," I admit. "But I was in the middle of a very posh restaurant."

"So you're getting married to Dante."

"I agreed for the benefit of the baby," I say primly.

She laughs. "Come on, this is me you're talking to. You are already half in love if not head over heels with him. Admit it!"

"Well, I don't know about love, but he has been very kind and thoughtful to me since I arrived."

"Kind and thoughtful? Pull the other one. You can't fool me, Rosa. I know you better than you know yourself. So what comes next?"

"We are flying to Avanti this weekend so his father and stepmother can meet me."

"The King and Queen," Star cries excitedly.

"Yeah," I say, feeling nervous all over again.

"Rosa, I'm so happy for you," Star coos.

"Star! I'm going to meet the king and queen and visit a real palace! And I don't know how to act. The closest I ever got to a Palace is watching the changing of the guards."

"Hey, it's you, remember. There is nothing you can't handle. Remember what that janitor told you in New York."

"Life, no matter what happens, is a wonderful adventure," I say softly.

"Exactly. Besides, I'm sure Dante will coach you on what to do and say."

" I still feel like I'm in a dream and I'll wake up at any moment."

"Well, unless we are dreaming the same dream, it's real."

"Star, I could talk all night about what happened to me today, but I'm so tired I can hardly keep my eyes open."

"It's three in the afternoon. Why are you so tired?"

"I don't know, but in the last two weeks I get really exhausted really fast."

"Don't worry. I think that is normal with some women. Okay, go to bed, but I want you to call me as soon as you wake up. I need more details and updates and eventually pictures! Lots of pictures of the palace."

"Okay, Star."

"Sleep tight, Rosa. I am so happy for you."

I hang up, walk to the bed and fall into a deep sleep.

CHAPTER 24

Rosa

"*P*lease, Dante, don't drive so wildly this time," I say as I climb into the Ferrari. "I'm a little bit out of sorts this morning."

"Morning sickness?"

"No, nerves. It's all happening too fast for me and I'm nervous about meeting your father."

He grins wolfishly. "Don't worry, unlike me, my father won't bite."

I slap his arm. "Very funny."

"Relax, Rosa. You don't need anybody's approval, but if you wanted to work a bit harder to get my approval I wouldn't object."

"Stop it," I wail.

He reaches across the console and squeezes my knee."Oh, baby. You're not marrying my father. You're marrying me."

"It's fine for you to say that. Of course, I want your father to approve of me. Don't you want my mum to approve of you?"

He shrugs. "Not really."

"That's because you know she's going to approve of you," I say, annoyed that he doesn't understand. "Your father is a king. He probably has very high expectations for the woman who marries you and I don't even know what I'm supposed to do when I meet him. Do I curtsy or what?"

"Rosa, do you trust me?"

"Yes."

"Then relax. Everything will be fine. I don't want you to behave in any other way than how you normally do, okay? And no, I don't want you curtsying to him or anybody else. We are all equal. His blood is not purer than yours."

"But—"

"No buts. We will never be called upon to undertake any royal duties so we will just behave like ordinary people. We are just there to have fun and for me to introduce you to my father and Linnea."

"I don't even know how to address them."

"His majesty."

I swallow. "See, I didn't even know that and you never even told me until I asked you. What else don't I know?"

"Look we have two hours on the plane. Use that time to ask me anything you want, okay?"

"Okay."

Dante steps on the gas pedal, and the Ferrari comes forth and races like a cheetah after an impala across the savanna. Except it is Dante flying through the narrow streets, weaving in and out of traffic at spine-chilling speed.

"Are you sure Sergio will pick up my bags and bring them to the plane?" I ask, hanging on to the door.

"Yes, he's very reliable," Dante says glancing at me.

"No, no watch the road," I shout.

The screeching of tires anounces the end of our ride. A single Lear Jet is parked on the tarmac.

"We aren't going to the terminal?"

"No."

I look at what appears like a coat of arms painted on the side of the plane. "That's your family plane?"

"No, it's mine and I will pilot it myself," he tells me.

I turn to look at him in horror. "You're not going to fly that thing, are you?"

"I promise you I am a very good pilot. Top of my class, actually. You will be perfectly safe."

"No," I say shaking my head. "If you are going to fly like you drive, I'm going commercial."

Dante smiles. "How cute you are. I never know what's going to come out of your pretty mouth."

"Very loud screams if you plan to fly us," I grumble.

"Trust me, it'll be the smoothest flight you've ever had," he assures me suavely. I stare out of the windscreen marvelling at how my life has changed while he climbs out of the car and comes around to open the door for me. "Come along, I'll show you my little toy."

"If you crash that thing and I die, I'll … I'll haunt you for eternity," I warn as he takes my hand and pulls my reluctant body out of the deep seat.

"Deal," he murmurs, pulling me close to his body.

His body is warm and his hands are sure and strong. I look

into his face. In the sunlight he looks like a stunning Greek statue. Every line perfect. I want to suck his sensuous lips into my mouth, and consume him … drink him in.

I turn my face away so he will not see how smitten I am with him. I pretend to look back at the seat and frown. "Soon I'll be so big, I won't be able to get out of your car on my own."

"When that happens, we'll use the Bentley and I'll put one of those corny 'Pregnant Woman Aboard' stickers on the bumper," he teases, his breath warm against my neck. I step away from him and we walk toward the plane's boarding ramp, where to my relief a man in a pilot's uniform and a stewardess are standing at attention. Maybe he was messing with me.

"Tell me that is a pilot I see?"

"That is a pilot you see."

"So you're not going to fly the plane?" I ask hopefully.

"Sorry, he's my co-pilot."

Suddenly I feel the backs of my eyes burn and I stop walking.

Dante stops too. "What's the matter, *bella*?"

"I … I … uh … don't know," I say, tears flowing down my cheeks. "I'm never like this. I'm usually so strong and practical. It must be all the hormones going crazy in my system, but I think I actually preferred it when you were just another smooth-talking bastard."

"Oh, baby," he says gently, wiping my cheeks with his fingers. "I'm still the same cocky bastard. None of this is important."

I look up into his eyes. In the sunlight they are molten-gold and hypnotic. I could look into them forever. "I'm not ready to meet your parents."

"When you learned to swim, did you put one toe in first then another bit, and another bit, or did you jump in all at once?"

GEORGIA LE CARRE

"All at once," I reply.

"I thought so. You will not meet a single person in the palace that will be better than you. You won't need the approval of anyone. Not even my father's. Just be yourself and you'll charm everybody. Besides, I'll be next to you the whole time. Nothing bad will happen."

I sniff.

"Do you trust me?"

I nod slowly. I never thought I'd say it and mean it, but I do trust him. Completely.

"That's my girl," he says, taking my hand and leading me forward.

Dante nods at the man wearing the captain's uniform. "Morning, Captain. Is the flight plan turned in and everything set with customs?"

"Everything is ready, Your Highness. Once you are onboard, we'll be on our way. Will you be piloting the plane on this trip?"

I hold my breath. Please don't say yes.

Dante glances at me and smiles slowly. "No," he says still looking at me.

We ascend the stairs and enter the jet. It's like walking into a luxurious long room with leather sofas and cabinets with crystal glasses.

"Would you like a drink before we take off?" the stewardess asks with a smile as she stands over us.

I want to ask for a double shot of vodka. I feel like I am going to need a very stiff drink, but I smile and ask for a glass of juice. Dante orders the same and the stewardess brings two glasses of juice and sets them on the table in front of us.

"To us," Dante says lifting his glass.

I touch mine to his. "To think that all this time, I never knew that I was just a little girl frog in a big pond waiting for a prince to come along and kiss me, and turn me into a princess."

Dante laughs.

I look at him laughing and I know I'm doing the right thing. "You know what, Dante? If you really want to pilot this plane you can. I do trust you."

He stops laughing and something changes in his eyes. For a moment it looks as if he is going to say something important, then he shakes his head, and the moment is gone.

"Captain Anderson is ready for you in the cockpit, Your Highness," the stewardess says.

"Thank you, Elsa," Dante says. "Please tell the Captain to call me if he needs me."

"Relax, bella. I'm not leaving your side," Dante says as he straps the seatbelt around my waist.

"Tell me everything I need to know about your family."

For an hour he describes for me all kinds of little details about his family and life in the palace for which I am very grateful, but then I feel that familiar tiredness come over me.

"You look rather tired, my darling. Lay your head in my lap. I'll massage your head until you fall asleep."

I lay my head in his lap, and true to his word, Dante begins to run his fingers through my hair.

"*W*ake up, sleeping beauty. We've arrived," Dante says.

"What … Where …" I ask sitting up, still in a sleepy fog. "You mean we are in …"

"Avanti," he supplies, motioning to the window. "Look for yourself."

I move over to the end of the sofa and glance out the window of the jet. It takes me a moment to assimilate what I am seeing. It's a black Mercedes Limo with flags bearing the same coat of arms that is painted on the side of the jet, and a convoy of eight motorcycle outriders with drivers wearing bright red and blue uniforms.

"All this for you!" I exclaim.

"Royalty has its privileges." His voice is light, but I catch an undertone.

I shake my head, still unable to wrap my mind around the fact that Dante is not an ordinary man. He is royalty.

"Yes, and I must warn you in advance that there will be people lining the streets to greet us as we pass," he says.

CHAPTER 25

Rosa

I take a deep breath. I tell myself I can do this, but the level of nervousness I feel is foreign to me. It's not the knowledge that I will step off the jet and enter an entirely different world than I am accustomed to. New things do not scare me. I went to the big apple on my own right after college. I just upped and left. Never hesitated for a second.

For some strange reason I feel almost afraid to leave this plane. My antenna is up. As if there is something dangerous waiting for me out there. Which is so weird, because in essence, we're going to spend the weekend at his mom and dad's place. It's not even like they live in the middle of some warzone. They live in the most civilized place on earth. In a palace.

I squash the uneasy feeling knowing that once I step off this plane nothing will ever be the same again. "It's just another adventure, Rosa."

"Sorry. I didn't catch that," Dante says.

I smile up at him. "Nothing, just mumbling to myself."

"Shall we?" he asks holding out his hand.

I take it and we start moving towards the door. The captain and stewardess are standing stiffly by the door.

"Good job, Captain, as always," Dante says.

"Thank you, Your Highness," the captain says bowing his head as we walk past.

I can't help but notice that he's acting differently toward Dante now that we're in Avanti. I think Dante wasn't completely honest with me. Looks like the people of Avanti take their royals very seriously.

The walk down the stairs to the tarmac is one I will never forget. There are cameras clicking and paparazzi moving around behind ropes jostling for a better angle calling out to Dante and, to my surprise, even me.

"Dante, Dante. When's the wedding? Hey, Rosa, give us a smile, Rosa. What does it feel like, Rosa?"

A smartly-dressed newswoman is doing a standup in front of her cameraman. She is speaking in a rapid-fire language that sounds a bit like German, as she motions toward me and Dante.

"Welcome to the royal fishbowl," Dante whispers as he leans his head toward me.

"Yeah, Prince Charming, you sort of left this part out," I say, as I plaster a smile on my face.

"Don't worry. It's just the national press. They're all riled up because they've got wind of my impending marriage and want to know if I have changed my mind about resuming my duties as Crown Prince."

"And have you?"

"No. Finding you has made me even more determined not to carry on with that outdated system."

A group of men dressed in colorful uniforms and wearing strangely shaped helmets—similar to those worn by the Swiss Guard at the Vatican—stand at attention while Dante and I walk past.

A man in a dark suit is holding the limo door open for us. Star is never going to believe this. Heck. I don't even believe it myself, I think as I climb into the car. As he closes it, I see the motorcycle outriders move into position, two ahead, two on each side, and the last two behind the limo. I feel like Cinderella in her magical carriage on the way to the ball.

I thought Dante was joking when he told me there would be people lining the route to greet us, but there they are, waving flags, cheering, and shouting greetings to Dante as the royal procession of cars drives past.

Overwhelmed by all the fuss and attention, I gaze at their faces curiously. They are really excited to welcome their Prince home. We pass the city which reminds me of Prague. The roofs are all bright orange and the buildings either white or soft pastels. The balconies are filled with bright summer flowers. My first impression is of a very wealthy, well-maintained city.

"That's our cathedral," Dante says, pointing to a tall structure.

I lift my chin and look up at the marvelous stone building.

The limo turns a corner, and down at the end of the two-lane street, lined with beautiful trees, the palace rises up into the sky. Like something straight out of a Disney movie, except it is larger, much larger and more magnificent. Snow white with ostentatious, intricate moldings, it looks like it could have been fashioned out of ice. The summer sun falls on the hundreds of windows making them reflect light like shards of glass. I stare at the gold-domed tower and turrets with amazement. This is exactly how I imagined a palace would look when I was a child.

Tearing my eyes away from all that splendor I glance across the seat at Dante. "Just an ordinary family sitting around watching TV, huh?"

He shrugs and smiles. "Can you blame me? I was trying to calm my bride's jittery nerves. Though I might not have been totally forthcoming, quite frankly, watching TV in a five hundred room palace is no different than watching it in a three bedroom house." He actually looks serious.

As the vehicle pulls around the huge fountain with water spouting all around a massive copper statue of a knight mounted on a horse, I see livered staff standing in line waiting for our arrival. Hell, it is like a scene from a movie.

I glance at Dante, and feel the stirrings of apprehension. Will I be good enough for his parents?

He squeezes my hand. "I realize it is all new to you, but trust me, you'll get used to it in no time."

Both our doors are opened at the same time. I get out and glance over the top of the car at Dante for guidance of what I should do next. He winks at me. At that moment a middle-aged woman in a dark blue dress steps out of the line. To my surprise, Dante strides up to her and envelopes her in a bear hug.

"Matilda," he says, stepping back. "You don't look a day over thirty."

"It's time you came back," she says softly. I can see tears in her eyes.

Dante frowns. "I'm not back. I'm just here for the weekend."

A look of sorrow passes her face.

Dante beckons me to join him so I walk around to him.

"Matilda, this is Rosa. My fiancée. Rosa, this is my nanny, Matilda Olsenberg."

Matilda turns her head and looks at me. I smile at her and she bows her head respectfully. Then she turns back to Dante and smiles. There is real happiness flashing in her eyes.

"Sometimes our fates are mapped out for us before we are born. You will be King of Avanti one day, Prince Nils." As soon as she finishes talking she drops into a deep curtsy.

Dante looks at me and shrugs.

A man at our side clears his throat. "Her Majesty has placed Miss Winchester in the Redwood suite. Of course, your rooms have been aired and are ready for you."

Dante's arm comes around my waist. "Thank you, Viggo. Those sleeping arrangements will be perfect."

Viggo nods politely.

"Where is my father?"

"He is in the South garden, Your Highness. He will meet you in the music room once you have settled in."

"Very good. Tell him I'll see him in half-an-hour."

"Certainly, Your Highness."

"Miss Winchester," a uniformed maid says as she steps forward. "If you would like to follow me. I'll show you to your rooms."

"Thank you, but that won't be necessary. I'll take my fiancée to her quarters myself," Dante says smoothly.

"What about my luggage?" I ask.

"One of the staff will fetch it to your quarters," Viggo says quietly.

I thank him and Dante exerts a little pressure on the small of my back. We start walking towards the entrance.

"Looks like we'll be sleeping in different parts of the palace," I say as I follow him across the lawn to the entrance of the palace.

Dante looks down at me, his face amused. "Don't worry. It's walking distance."

Two guards, also dressed in colorful uniforms, stare straight ahead, and don't change expressions as we walk past.

"My God. It feels so strange to completely ignore them like that."

"Again, you'll get use to the royal guards. Unfortunately, it's another one of the stupid traditions I detest."

"I don't like it either," I reply as we step into the palace entrance. My mouth drops open. "Wow! This is so very beautiful."

"I guess it is very beautiful, you forget after some time."

"I still can't believe you said your mother and father sit around watching television like normal families," I say as I try hard not to gawk at the vast spaces, the rich decorations, the massive portraits and ancient tapestries decorating the walls. After only a few turns I'm lost.

"God, Dante, I'll never be able to find my way back to my room once I leave it. This place is like a maze."

"It can be confusing at first, but you'll catch on quickly. It's not as complicated as it appears."

"Uh huh," I mock. "Maybe it's not confusing to you because you grew up crawling the halls in diapers. To me it's a maze."

"You've met Matilda. Can you see her letting me crawl around like some street urchin?" Dante asks cheerfully.

Dante stops in front of elaborate teakwood doors with the family coats of arms carved on the front. "The Redwood suite," he says, and pushes open the double doors.

CHAPTER 26

Rosa

*O*h, my God! I've visited some impressive homes and Nikolai, Star's billionaire husband, lives in one hell of an impressive mansion, but never in my wildest imagination could I envision something like this. First; the size. The room had to be easily larger than my entire flat back in London. Second; the beauty and luxury. One entire wall is made up of tall, narrow windows. Sunlight streams in through them and falls on the Princess bed. A fairytale canopy bed, draped in silks with lilac and gold stripes, and smaller strips of deep blue stretching up to each corner and surrounding the top of the bed.

The sheets are the snowiest imaginable. Four pillows in snowy cases line the top of the mattress. A blanket embroidered in gold is folded back and lies halfway down the mattress.

"Do you like the room?" Dante asks seemingly entertained by my reaction.

GEORGIA LE CARRE

"What's not to like? It's gorgeous." I walk toward the window.

Directly in front of me are painstakingly manicured formal gardens with their precise rows of flowering plants. I see three gardeners hard at work to keep it utterly immaculate. Beyond the city are rolling hills scattered with cottages that remind me of those one would expect to find in the Swiss Alps. One could never tire of a view like this no matter how often one saw it. I could stand here for hours. I'm overwhelmed already.

Dante comes to stand behind me. I lean back against his body. "Spectacular, isn't it?" he says, wrapping his arms around my waist.

"It is a very unfair world we live in. Some people are born to this and others are born starving in Africa."

He kisses the side of my neck and there is a catch in his voice. "It is the way of the world, *bella.*"

There's a soft knock on the door and Dante turns toward it.

"Miss Winchester's luggage is here, Your Highness," the maid announces from the doorway.

"Bring it in," Dante says, and a male servant brings my suitcase through the door.

Dante speaks to him in rapid Avantian, then turns to me, a scowl on his face. "Rosa, would you mind if I leave you and go to see my horse. He's too old to ride now, but he is bonded to me, and he is not very well. It will make him happy to see me again."

"Yes, of course, go see him. I'll be fine. I'm still exploring my room!" I say.

"I will introduce you to him tomorrow," he says, coming over and kissing me gently on my forehead.

"Please don't worry about me. Go see your horse."

After he strides out of the room, the maid who had been

152

hanging around the door speaks up. "Would you like for me to unpack for you, Miss Winchester?"

"Thank you, but that won't be necessary as I didn't pack very much."

"My name is Elsa and if you need me for anything at all you can call me by pressing this button," she says pointing to one of the buttons hidden under a bit of swirling material over the bed.

I thank her and she starts to walk out, then stops, and curtsys. "The clothes in your suitcase must be creased by now, I'd be happy to steam them for you."

I smile. "You know what, Elsa. I'd love some help unpacking. Thank you."

She smiles back, then goes to my suitcase and carrying it, opens the door to a walk-in closet that would make the Kardashians envious. My meager possessions will hardly make a dent. I see myself reflected again and again down the length of the closet.

"If you need to refresh yourself while I put away your belongings, Miss Winchester," Elsa says pointing to another door.

"Thanks, and please call me, Rosa."

She looks shocked. "Oh, that would not be proper, Miss Winchester."

No wonder Dante ran away from all this rigid adherence to tradition and regulations. Shaking my head, I step into the bathroom. The counters are covered in gleaming white and black marble. There are two matching sinks, each with—can they be real gold faucets? Inside my own head, I utter a few more "wows." A mammoth Jacuzzi bath stands to one side, and in another corner is a massive shower.

By the time I freshen up and come out Elsa has finished unpacking my luggage. "Unless there's anything else, Miss

Winchester, I will go and steam these clothes, and arrange for your ball gown to be professionally taken care of tonight."

I give her a grateful smile. "Nothing else, Elsa. Thank you. I appreciate your help."

Elsa closes the door behind her and I have to go up on tip toes to reach the top of the bed. The mattress sinks under me. I have never slept in a bed this sumptuous. I run my fingers lightly on the silky embroidered thread. Star and Cindy will die when I tell them about all this. Just as I am about to call Star, I hear a knock on the door.

"Who is it?" I call.

"Cassandra. May I come in?"

Cassandra. It must be Dante's sister-in-law. "Of course," I say, and hurry towards the door, but before I have a chance to reach it, a beautiful woman rushes inside. She grabs me around the waist and leaning forward, kisses both my cheeks.

"Rosa," she says, "it is so nice to meet you at last."

"At last?" I echo. To be honest I'm stunned by her extraordinary friendliness after the formal way everyone else in the palace has behaved.

She steps back and gives me a sparkling smile. She's a slender woman maybe a few years younger than I am. Her hair is pale blonde, and her complexion is creamy. She is wearing a knee-length dark green silk dress with a pattern of yellow roses. I recognize it instantly as this year's summer collection from Gucci.

"Yes. I've been wondering about the woman who could enchant Dante so much that he's now ready to get married and settle down."

"Enchant? That's a quaint word I hardly ever hear anymore."

She wrinkles her nose charmingly. "Perhaps there is a better word. I directly translated the word we use in Avantian. Should I have used the word hook instead?"

I grin. "No. don't use that word. It makes Dante sound like a fish."

She giggles. "I heard you're the new editor of *Fashion Rome*. It is one of my favorite magazines."

"I'm afraid I've been the editor for such a short time, I haven't done a single thing yet."

"I'm sure you'll do a great job … that is, if you continue."

"What do you mean?"

She looks surprised. "Surely, you won't continue with the magazine after you and Dante get married, will you?"

"Yes, I will. I want to work and Dante is fine with that."

Her eyebrows rise. "Oh." Then she smiles suddenly. "We need to sit down and have a good gossip session."

Slightly taken aback, I stare at her. This is a princess, and she wants to gossip. She carries on looking at me expectantly so I motion in the direction of a nest of sofas and chairs, not really expecting her to take up my offer, but she immediately crosses in front of me and floats down into one of the winged chairs. I follow her and sit at one end of the sofa.

"So tell me all about how you met," she invites.

My eyes widen at her directness.

"You'll get used to me. Everyone eventually does, though it takes some people a lot of time."

I laugh. "Yes, Dante told me about you."

She leans forward eagerly. "What did he say?"

"Well, for one thing, he said you bring a breath of fresh air to the palace."

"He said that, did he? That's very nice of him. And what else did he tell you about me?"

"That you're sassy."

She throws back her head and laughs. "An apt description, I must say." Then she becomes serious. "So come on. Tell me about how you met Dante, but most of all how you managed to tame him when no other woman could."

"Well, I don't know that I've tamed him."

She gives me a meaningful look. "I watched you arriving from my window and he looked pretty tame to me."

"He did?"

She nods. "It is common knowledge that Dante sowed a lot of wild oats in his time and you've put an end to all of it." She glances at me more closely. "In the beginning, I had a choice between the two brothers, but I couldn't be hacked with someone as wild as Dante. I mean, I would never be able to relax. What if he went back to his old ways? No, Linnus is much more my speed. Besides I wasn't that special person to make a man like Dante stop whoring and settle down."

I touch my stomach. "Well, I don't think I am either, but he really wants to make this work for the sake of the child."

"It doesn't matter why, I'm just so glad you're going to be a part of the family." Even though we are the only people in the room she leans forward and whispers conspiratorially. "Linnus's parents are so stuffy. It's like they are caught in a time warp."

"But I read they are one of the most progressive royal families in Europe."

"No, that is not a word I would use on them. Not that I dislike either one of them. Far from it. I like them very much, but they wouldn't know what progressive was if it sat up and slapped them with a wet fish."

"Oh! Can you tell me about them? What they're like?"

Her eyes run down my body. "They'll like you; I'm certain of it, though neither of them likes to show any emotion in public. When I first got here I wondered if they had sex with all their clothes on."

My eyes widen. I definitely did not want to gossip about Dante's parents in this way. "I suppose they have their traditions and responsibilities to live up to."

"You can say that again. They certainly keep their traditions going." She laughs. "Just promise me something."

"What?"

"Once you're married to my brother-in-law, please don't change and become like everyone else in this palace."

"I'll certainly try." I look into her eyes. "Seems you managed that just fine."

"I'd like to think so. I'll kill myself before I become one of the walking dead around here."

I laugh. "If you don't mind my asking are you also from a royal background?"

"I don't mind at all." She sighs. "My father is a Count."

"A Count?"

"Minor royalty, I suppose. But my father never much considered that important." She raises her eyes to meet mine. "I hope you don't hold it against me."

I gaze at her surprised. "Why would I do such a thing?"

"Inverse snobbery is very fashionable these days. Talking about fashion, how would you like to go shopping tomorrow afternoon?"

"Shopping?"

"Why not? Avanti is a tiny country, but we have excellent stores. Nearly anything you'd ever want is right here."

"Uh … it's just I don't know what plans Dante has made."

She laughs as if I have said something really funny. "Dante wouldn't have made any plans for tomorrow afternoon. He knows that you have to get ready for the ball." She frowns. "Did you bring something for the ball?"

"Yes, I brought a dress."

She springs up. "Show me."

I go to the walk-in closet with her following closely behind. I open the cupboard and take out my dress. It's made of black lace, with floral appliqués across the bodice.

She frowns. "Well, it's very nice, but I'm afraid it won't be grand enough. You're the guest of honor."

I look at the dress that I had thought would be perfect because of its simplicity.

"Don't worry. I know just the place we can get something awesome for you."

I take my time hanging the dress back in the closet while I decide what is the best way to handle the situation. Judging by the fact that she is wearing the latest Gucci dress while she is technically at home, a shopping expedition with her will definitely be more expensive than I can afford. I turn back. "I … er … "

"What?" she asks, her bright eyes round with curiosity.

To my relief, I am saved by a knock at the door. "Rosa, are you there?" Dante calls.

We walk back into the bedroom. "Yes, come on in."

"Hey, Cassandra," Dante says as he walks in.

"It is good to see you again, Dante."

"Likewise." He turns to me. "You okay?"

"Yeah. Cassandra and I are just becoming acquainted"

"I'm trying to persuade your fiancée to take a shopping trip with me tomorrow afternoon. We need to get her a suitable ball gown, but she is reluctant because she doesn't know what you have planned for her."

He turns to look at me. "Yes, go get something lovely for yourself. Just put everything on my account."

Cassandra winks at me. "See how easy that was. Right. I'll see you at 2 p.m. tomorrow?"

CHAPTER 27

Rosa

"*How's* your horse?" I ask as soon as the door closes.

"I didn't know if he would be distant with me because I haven't seen him in two years, but he was ecstatic to see me again." He takes my hand, and sitting on the sofa, tugs me into his lap.

I snuggle my face between his neck and shoulder, amazed at how perfect it feels to be so close to him. "So tell me how he reacted."

His arms circle my waist. "Even though he is sick, he was so excited to see me he was like a damn puppy. He kept pawing the ground, neighing, and trying to get up on his hind legs."

I look up into his eyes. "Will he get better?"

He nods. "I think so."

"Good." I wriggle to get comfortable.

"Are you looking for trouble, young lady?" he asks lazily.

I stop wriggling. "No. I was trying to get comfortable. You are too hard."

"Damn right. I'm hard. I've got your delicious bottom on my dick."

I look up at him from beneath my lashes. Sometimes I still can't believe that I'm with Dante. "You know we can't do it now. Anyone could walk in on us."

He sighs. "Yeah, it's one of the worst things about living in the palace. Staff every-fucking-where you look."

I shrug. "The staff thing doesn't bother me, but the way people treat you is different than I expected."

"In what way?"

"Captain Anderson, for instance. His attitude towards you back in Rome was that of a pilot addressing his employer, but once we landed here, I noticed he was much more subservient to you."

He shrugs. "It didn't really occur to me, but I suppose it's because they refuse to accept that I have given up the title of Crown Prince."

I let my finger slide down his throat. "You gave up being a Prince to become a playboy in Rome?"

"Not exactly. I guess I was rebelling. I wanted to get away from all of it."

"I'm not sure I understand."

"Can we talk about this later? It's almost time for dinner and dinner is always formal so we'll have to get dressed."

"I brought something formal."

"Good. There are a couple of other things I need to tell you."

"Like what?"

"Dinner time protocol."

"You mean I won't be able to eat my peas with my knife?"

He grins. "I would have loved to have seen that, but since peas are never served except as a cream soup …"

I nod. "And even I know better than to eat my soup with a knife."

"You will be meeting my parents over aperitifs. I will introduce you to my stepmother first. Give her a small curtsy, she likes that, but don't make it theatrical. Cassandra calls her Linny, but do not use that nickname, unless she asks you to. Address her as Her Majesty."

"What's your stepmother like?"

He doesn't have to think. "Cold. She's a very cold woman."

"Oh." I look at him surprised. "You don't like her?"

"I don't know her. Less than a year after my father married her, I was sent off to live with my uncle."

"Why were you sent to live with your uncle?"

"Because my father didn't want the trouble. When he married Linea she was already pregnant with Linnus and I guess he just wanted a new start. He didn't want reminders of his old life and I was a big reminder. I have her eyes and hair color."

"How old were you then?"

"Seven." There is no sadness, no expression at all in his face, but in my mind's eyes I can see him as a small child. How confusing it must have been for him to lose his mother and then be abandoned by his father. All the wealth and splendor must have seemed like a mockery.

"I see," I say thoughtfully. Looks like there may be undercurrents of resentment running deep in this family.

"When you are first introduced to my father," Dante continues, "just bow from the neck. I'm not sure if he will or not, but he may shake your hand. At any rate let them make the first move."

"I can do that."

"You'll also meet my brother, Linnus, who is about your age. No need for formalities there. He's not a stickler for tradition and will probably shake hands. You've already met Cassandra."

I nod. "I liked her."

"After this a servant will escort you to your chair and seat you. Thank him with a nod, nothing more."

"Sounds simple, so far."

"Usually, there is little conversation during the meal. However, my parents may ask you a few questions. Answer them directly and simply. Once the final plate has been cleared we will head to the drawing room where coffee will be served. There could be some lively discussions, often led, as you probably guess, by Cassandra."

"All right."

"Anything you want to ask?"

"Nope, I will most probably keep my head down and say little."

"If you forget to do some of the things I told you it's no big deal, okay?"

"Okay."

There is a knock on the door and Dante sighs. "God, I remember now how much I hate palace life. There is simply no privacy at all."

"Yes?" I say.

"It's Elsa. I came to help you dress for dinner ... if that's satisfactory."

"Someone is going to help me to dress?" I whisper.

"Don't worry, I'll help you undress," he says with a wicked smile.

I scramble out of his lap. "Er … of course, Elsa. Come on in."

She opens the door and enters holding aloft my freshly pressed clothes. She curtsys and bows her head respectfully when she spots Dante. "I'll just hang these clothes up." Head bent she makes for the closet.

Dante unfurls himself from the sofa. "I'll come by a few minutes before 8 p.m. to escort you to the dining room."

"Okay, see you then."

He gives me a kiss on the cheek and walks to the door. "Everything will be fine. You'll see."

"May I ask you something, Elsa?" I say when she comes back into the room.

"Of course, Miss Winchester."

"How on earth do you plan to help a twenty-six-year old adult dress?"

Elsa giggles then covers her mouth in mortification at her own lack of decorum. "I'm sorry."

"Elsa. I'm not a Princess. Please can you relax and just be normal around me."

"My job is to fetch things and help you with your hair," she says primly.

I sigh. I'm not going to get through to her.

"Which dress would you like to wear tonight?" she asks.

"The blue one."

"It is the nicest one," she says softly.

I smile at her. "Thank you. I spent a long time choosing it, and I love it."

Certainly, I have never bought something so expensive. It is even more expensive than the ball gown since I didn't know how much use I would get out of that, but I knew I'd use this one many times. I so blew two months of salary on it. The floor-length, sleeveless, structured Alexander McQueen has a slit in the back, which means the velvet dress could follow the shape of my body from neck to toe.

Elsa carefully removes the dress from the wooden hanger and helps me pull it over my head. She straightens it here and there before sliding up the hidden zipper in the back.

"You look very beautiful in it," she says sincerely.

I turn and look at my side profile in the mirror and decide I am happy with what I see. Elsa helps me put my hair up. Then I paint my face and don a pair of dark blue velvet heels. Once Elsa leaves, I realize I still have half-an-hour to kill before Dante comes to take me down to dinner. Instead of sitting around stewing I call Star.

"Guess what?" she cries excitedly.

"What?"

"We'll be flying into Switzerland tomorrow. Nikolai has a business meeting. I'll just be across the border from you. Shall we meet up on Sunday?"

"Yes, absolutely. I'd love to see you again."

"Great. I'll talk to Nikolai and find out what his schedule is like. Even if he can't join us we can still meet up. I am dying to hear everything that is happening with you. Besides, I want to see how much your belly has grown."

I laugh. "You'll be very disappointed. It has not grown at all."

"No?"

"Sorry. Although, wearing the dress I am in tonight I am glad it hasn't."

"Oh, are you in your Alexander McQueen?"

"Just about. It is a bit tight around the belly, but if I don't eat too much and suck it in all night it'll be all right."

She laughs. "Oh, Rosa. I just can't wait to see your baby."

"You'll laugh, but I've started to really want it too. I mean like really want it. The other day I even thought of taking a year off and just enjoying being a mother."

"Well, quite frankly. You can be an editor anytime, but that first year in a baby's life is so precious. If you miss something it will be gone forever."

"Let's see what happens. I won't decide anything right now."

"Hang on, someone is calling me."

"Listen just go, because I have to call Cindy, or she has sworn never to speak to me again."

I ring off and FaceTime Cindy. It's her day off so she kicks off her shoes, and orders me to tell her everything, which I gladly do. The time flies while I regale her with all my news. Before I know it, Dante is knocking lightly on the door. "Got to go. I'll call you when I get back to Rome. Mwaaaah."

"Bye baby. Have a wonderful time," she sings before I ring off.

CHAPTER 28

Rosa

*S*o it's time to meet the parents. The butterflies take residence once more in my tummy. "Come in," I call.

Dante opens the door, then stops in his tracks. My mouth dries at the sight of him. If Dante is not the most beautiful man on earth, I don't know who is. In a dark suit he is enigmatic and mysterious.

"Jesus, Rosa. You expect me to sit through dinner while you look like that?"

"What are you talking about? I am totally covered."

"Oh fuck! You have no idea. That dress just screams fuck me."

"Stop being such a pervert. This dress does not scream fuck me."

"Everything you wear screams fuck me."

I lick my lips. "Well, if you come around after dinner I could do something about your affliction."

"You could?"

"I'm sure I could prescribe something that could take away the pain."

His smile is very wicked. "Thank you, Doctor Winchester."

"You're welcome, Your Royal Highness."

He holds his arm out. "Ready?"

I slip my arm through his.

Rather than turning left as we come out the door and retracing the steps we'd taken to reach my room, Dante leads me to the right, down a hallway with carpeting so thick I feel like I'm sinking into it. It's a dark blue while the walls are more the color of a morning sky. Various official-looking portraits hang on the walls, all beautifully painted and displayed in elaborately carved and gilded frames.

Dante turns to look at me. "Nervous?"

"A little, well, a lot."

"Just be yourself and remember: anytime you feel intimidated just think of them sitting on a toilet."

I smile at him. "Thank you."

At the bottom of a gracefully curving staircase we enter what looks like the lobby of a very expensive hotel. The walls are adorned with a reddish-gold fleur-de-lis pattern on an off-white background. On strategically placed plinths sit marble statues of human figures and animals. One that catches my attention is a marble statue of a doe with her head held high as if listening for any danger that may endanger the fawn lying at her feet.

Dante notices my fascination.

"That's one of my favorites too," he tells me. "As a small boy, I used to wonder what the mother deer was listening for."

I turn to him. "That is beautiful. I think I would have loved to have known Dante the boy."

He smiles and leads me across the room to another hallway. We enter another vast, richly decorated room where I see a couple in their early fifties sitting opposite each other. One glance is enough to know they don't love each other.

The man has dark brown hair and a moustache that slants downward at the corners of his mouth. Like the woman beside him, he seems too thin. He is wearing a black suit and a soft blue shirt. The woman is slender, almost emaciated, with rich blonde shoulder-length hair. She is wearing an emerald-green, full-length gown and a pearl necklace. Diamonds shine in her earlobes.

"Linnea," Dante says politely as we go up to them. "It is my pleasure to introduce Rosa Winchester to you." He turns to me. "Rosa, I present Her Majesty, Queen Linnea of Avanti."

I curtsy.

"It is a pleasure to meet you," she says, extending a smooth, narrow hand towards me. She smiles, and I'm struck by how it doesn't reach her chilly gray eyes.

"The pleasure is all mine," I murmur as she withdraws her hand and clasps her other hand over it.

Dante exerts gentle pressure on the small of my back and turns me slightly to my left.

"Father this is Rosa. Rosa, meet my father, His Majesty, the King of Avanti."

I bow my head as Dante had instructed.

"Welcome to Avanti," his father says. "I hope you are enjoying your stay."

"Thank you very much, Your Majesty. You have a beautiful pala ... home."

He smiles and reaching forward takes my right hand in both

of his. His grip is weak and reminds me of the clutch of a very old man. Startled, I stare at him. I can feel the queen narrow her eyes with surprise and displeasure.

He withdraws his hands. "I am glad my son found you. I can see now why he is so enamored of you."

Thankfully, I am saved from answering as Cassandra enters the room with a man I presume to be Dante's brother, though there seems to be little resemblance to him. While Dante is tall and broad, his brother Riccardo has more of a wrestler's build with an angular face and sly eyes. His hair is light brown with an almost reddish tint.

Cassandra makes a funny face, and I can't help but smile back.

Dante turns to me. "You've already met Cassandra, and this is my brother Linnus. Linnus, my fiancée, Rosa Winchester."

"A pleasure," he says, giving me a wide smile.

"Likewise," I reply.

Cassandra throws her arms around my waist and kisses me on the cheek. "Again, welcome to Avanti, Rosa. I am so glad you're here."

"I'm glad to be here," I tell her, slightly embarrassed.

"Well, shall we be seated?" the queen says coldly.

Servants appear as if from nowhere to seat everyone at the table. Then begins a seven-course meal—first a spicy cucumber salad with anchovy butter and crushed new potatoes. Throughout the meal, as Dante predicted, there is almost no talking. After the sea bass with fennel and spicy grape relish, is slow-roasted pork ribs with membrillo glaze, followed by lamb steaks. Every course is cooked to perfection.

Cassandra, seated on my left, leans toward me. "What do you think?" she asks.

What I think is; I'm so stuffed I don't know if I can even get out of my chair, but what I say is, "Absolutely delicious. Especially those lamb steaks with yeast butter and warm hummus. It's not like this every day, is it?"

"It's like this *every day*," she says flatly.

My eyes widen. "How on earth do you stay so slim?"

Cassandra throws back her head and laughs. "Simple. Take only half of what you want and eat half of what you take."

"But what a waste."

"The staff will eat it," she says airily.

"Is the food to your satisfaction?" Dante's father asks from across the table.

"It's delicious."

"I'm glad you approve so heartily," he says with a smile.

"I certainly do."

"So," the queen says, "I understand you are originally from London."

"Yes, I am. You have an accent that is not Avantian, is it?"

"No, I am of Austrian and German ancestry," she admits.

"It's a wonderful accent," I tell her.

"I used to love to hear her talk," Dante's father says. He glances at her. "I don't mean that I no longer like to hear her. I'll always want to hear her talk ..." he trails off. There's an almost sad smile on his face. "Actually, I think I'd better stop talking before I get myself into hot water."

The queen glances in his direction, her eyes filled with barely concealed impatience. He returns her look, then laughs, and takes a sip of his wine.

"Don't drink too much, darling. It will interfere with your ... supplements," she admonishes.

He puts his glass back down on the table. "You're right, of course, my darling. Can't have anything interfering with my … supplements."

Astounded by the odd exchange, I glance at Dante. He is staring at his father with a strange expression. If this is Cassandra's idea of 'stuffy', I wonder what 'unstuffy' would be. I look over at my future sister-in-law who simply raises her eyebrows and shrugs at me. I gather from that what I've witnessed isn't typical behavior.

"So, Rosa," the king says, "what has Dante told you about our country?"

"Not a great deal," I answer slowly. "I know that the economy is based on being a tax haven."

"It is, indeed, but mostly because we have been fortunate enough as to attract some of the richest people in the world to live in our country. There are more billionaires per-square foot here then there are anywhere else in the world," Linnus says proudly.

"Really?" I say, impressed.

"Though you may hardly have heard of our country, it's centuries old. Founded in the twelve hundreds, actually," the king says.

"I didn't realize that." I look over at Cassandra who rolls her eyes.

"Here we go," she mouths to me.

As she predicted he launches into a history which I find fascinating, but is obviously uninteresting to Cassandra. She pays little attention, and even has to stifle a yawn. Maybe she's heard it all before—or even learned about it in school. Whatever the reason she is very bored.

Cassandra leans forward and whispers into my ear, "I told you. Stuffy, stuffy, stuffy."

I don't react, but I actually feel bad for Dante's father. I know he saw her whisper in my ear and maybe even heard what she said. He is the head of this household and yet Cassandra openly shows disrespect.

Dante pushes his chair back and stands. He turns to his father. "Thank you for a very enlightening explanation," he says. I can't tell if he's being sincere or not, but his voice is stiff and strained. I have never heard it like that before. "It was very helpful to Rosa and you've mentioned some things that I didn't even know."

The king nods. He appears exhausted and defeated.

"Shall we?" Dante says turning toward me.

I nod, and a servant arrives to pull back my chair.

"Goodnight," Dante says, addressing everyone. I echo his sentiment and there are murmurs all around the table.

Cassandra reminds me of our shopping trip and Dante takes my arm to guide me out. Once we're in the hallway, I turn toward him.

"What was that all about?"

"Palace politics. Stay out of it, Rosa. We won't be living here, thank God."

"Dante?"

He looks down at me and I can see that even though his voice is normal, his eyes are troubled. "Yes?"

"I liked your father. I thought he was nice."

He swallows, then smiles distantly. "I think he liked you too. Come on, I want to show you the view from the tower."

We walk to the tower in silence.

"Careful. These stairs are treacherous," Dante warns as we start climbing the winding steps."

173

When we get to the top of the tower I let out an unconscious gasp. The stars are shining brightly in the night sky above us and the lights of the city like a twinkling carpet beneath us. It is just magnificent. It is almost a shame to think only one family could enjoy this view.

I turn toward Dante. "It's simply breathtaking."

"Yes, Avanti is a very beautiful country. We'll see some of it tomorrow."

"I'd love that."

I search his face in the dim light. Ever since dinner he has been preoccupied. "Dante, can't you tell me what's wrong?"

"No, Rosa. I won't drag you into this mess. We will have our life which will be separate from my family. We will only visit if we have to. Perhaps the next time we come it will be for my father's funeral."

I freeze. "Is your father really ill?"

He gazes far into the horizon. "I don't know, but he didn't look well, did he?"

"No. I'm sorry."

"It's okay. My father and I are almost strangers. My best memories of him are while my mother was alive. He was a different man then. After he married Linnea he changed drastically." He scowls. "Let's not talk about them. Let me take you back to your room. You must be tired."

"I'm all right. I slept during the flight," I say, but he is already turning away and leading the way down. We walk next to each other in silence, passing corridors and grand rooms.

"Well, here we are," he says finally. "Your room."

I stare up at him, trying to gauge his mood. "Thank you. It was a very nice evening."

"I can make it even nicer," he says with a crooked smile.

"Oh?"

"You have no idea what kind of thoughts have been running through my head while following that slit in your dress up the tower stairs."

I feel heat spread through my body. "But you can't. It's *verboteni*."

His eyes widen. "You learned the word for taboo in Avantian?"

I bite my bottom lip. "And a few others too. Do you want to hear them?"

He opens my door, sweeps me into his arms, and carries me to my Princess bed. It is while he is making love to me that I realize: I'm head over heels in love with my Prince.

CHAPTER 29

Rosa

I get up alone in my Princess bed. I stretch and look at the phone clock. Dante said be ready by eight, but it is only 6.30 a.m. I left the shutters open last night and I can see that it is already light outside. The queasy feeling starts, but I see that Dante has left my biscuits on the ornate top of the bedside cabinet. Opening the packet, I sit up and nibble at the biscuits slowly until the feeling passes.

Right. Time to try out the Jacuzzi.

I lie back in sweet smelling suds and close my eyes. My mind starts replaying everything that happened last night. Part of me still can't believe that Dante and I are getting married. What had happened at the dinner table was weird. Maybe Dante is right. I shouldn't get involved. Last night was the best sex we've ever had. Perhaps because I realized I'm in love with him. Whatever the reason, it was amazing.

Eventually, when my fingers go all pruney, I get out and dry myself off with a big fluffy towel. I tie the quilted dressing gown I find hanging from a hook inside the bathroom door and walk into my closet. A girl could get used to this.

I glance at the few pieces of clothing hanging in the closet. I can't go far wrong if I team my lightweight trouser suit with my cream blouse with ruffles down the front. Cindy, who must have been working the night shift at the Casino, sends me a little video of a cute husky saying I love you. I send back the pictures I took of Avanti. I'm dressed and ready when I hear his knock at the door.

"Who is it?" I pretend to ask.

"Who do you think?" Dante replies.

I run across the room and throw open the door. The sight of Dante makes my heart sing with joy. Dressed in a pair of grey slacks and a knit shirt, and with his hair still wet from a shower, he makes me feel all gooey inside. He runs his gaze down my body quickly then juts his face forwards and taps his cheek with his fingers. With a shy smile, I stand on my tiptoes and kiss the cheek he tapped.

He catches me as I lean back. "Where do you think you're going young lady? Lips. Always end with the lips."

The kiss makes my toes curl. By the time he raises his head I feel breathless and giddy with excitement.

"Good morning," he says huskily.

"Good morning to you too," I whisper shakily.

His sensuous lips curl upwards. "Did you sleep well?"

"I did, thanks." I still can't stop staring at his gorgeous face.

"You look very fresh," I murmur.

He grins. "I was out horseback riding. It always puts me in a fine mood."

"I would have loved to have watched you ride."

He touches my nose. "I wanted you to sleep. Maybe after the baby is born?"

I nod shyly. "Okay."

"Want to have breakfast with me?"

I shake my head. "I had my magic biscuits."

He laughs. "We're on our own for breakfast so you can just drink a cup of coffee while I eat."

"Perfect."

We take the same route downstairs, except now we turn left at the bottom and enter a much smaller room than the one we were in last night. Sunlight bursts through the many windows and strikes the juice glasses on the table. It's going to be a beautiful day.

A servant holds a chair out for me, and another moves to seat Dante.

"Good morning," Dante says.

The servant bows. "Good morning, Your Highness." He glances my way and again bows. "Good morning, Miss Winchester."

Dante orders eggs, bacon, and toast. How he can possibly be hungry after last night's massive meal is beyond me.

"I'd like to take you to one of my favorite places in Avanti. The caves," he says.

"Caves?"

"The kind where we can leave everyone else outside and go in and spend some time alone."

"And what would we do when we're there?" I tease.

He laughs wickedly. "I'll show you when we get there, wench."

178

I beam at him. My heart feels as if it will burst with love. "Tell me about these wonderful caves."

"Actually, you'll find them extremely interesting. They have prehistoric paintings guaranteed to take your breath away. Afterwards, I thought we might stop and have a quick bite before I bring you back here so you can catch a nap. If you plan it well you can sneak another nap in between your shopping trip and the ball. That way you won't get too tired."

I stare at him. Maybe he really does care for me, after all. "I think you are full of great ideas today."

A servant approaches with a metal covered platter and he rubs his hands together. "Mmmm … bacon."

❄

I'm reminded of a trip our family took to Switzerland once. I was only little and my father was still alive then. He always had a great sense of adventure. I think I inherited that trait from him. He rented a car and drove my mother and me out of town. Aimlessly we travelled, enjoying the view and seeing the sights. Every time we came to a crossroads he would simply ask my mother or me which way we preferred. That trip is one of my happiest childhood memories. Less than two years later he was gone forever, and my mother and I never went abroad together again.

This ride seems almost the same, the lie of the land, the faces of the people, the animals in their greener than green pastures, the neat little houses. Avanti has to be one of the most beautiful countries on earth.

"It's so peaceful here," I say to Dante. "Almost like we're in a different world. One where there are no cares and no problems."

He turns toward me. "That's a surprising thing to say from a girl that relishes the rat race."

"I don't relish it."

"Admit it. You thought of taking the baby to work."

"I did not," I deny. "In fact, I've been thinking I might take a year off. Spend it with the baby."

He stares at me in astonishment.

"Can you keep your eyes on the road, please?" I holler in a panic.

He turns back to the road and does not say anything else. I breathe a sigh of relief. I'm actually not ready to discuss the way I feel about him or the baby yet.

We go down one country road after another, most of them narrow trails under canopies of green leaves. Eventually, we come to an area with a chain-link fence beyond which stands a stone building the size of a small cottage.

"Here we are," Dante says as he pulls up to a gate and presses a button. Soon, a young man wearing a guard's uniform comes hurrying toward us. As soon as he spots Dante his face lights up.

"Your Highness," he says. "Welcome, welcome. What a wonderful surprise. You're here to explore the caves."

"Well, 'explore' might no longer be the right word since I've been here so many times." He smiles at the young man.

"Ah, then, let's say you're here to visit the caves again."

"Yes, and to show them to my fiancée."

The man gawks at me in astonishment before opening the gate. We drive through and park off to the side.

"Just a short walk," Dante says as we start down a brick-lined path.

I look around me. Tall trees dot a series of rolling hills— pines and maples; the sky is pale blue and filled with soft white clouds. "What a wonderful place," I say with a sigh.

"Matilda used to bring me here for picnics. No one lives for miles around, and I used to roam the hills and the woods with one of the sons of the cook."

Dante slips his arm around my waist and stops for a moment. "You know when our child is a little older, we'll have to bring him here too. And later on, maybe his brother or sister too."

"Would you mind very much if our baby turns out to be a girl?"

He runs his hand through his hair, a stupid smile on his face. "The only thing I care about is for our child to be born healthy."

"Me too," I whisper, and he smiles into my eyes. A special smile as if we are sharing the most wonderful secret in the world. We walk a little more and I feel as if I am floating on air with sheer happiness.

"Here we are," he says and points straight ahead. "The first of the three caves."

"Does no one ever come here?"

"Sometimes, on weekends or holidays, but I suppose to most people it's old hat. I just never seem to tire of the place." He releases his arm from around my waist and grabs my hand. "Come on," he says and starts pulling me along and running toward the entrance. I laugh and do my best to keep up with him. To be honest I'm surprised by his mood. He reminds me of a small boy eager to show me his discovery.

He stops just inside the entrance. It is dark and it takes my eyes some time to adjust to the sudden dimness.

"Don't worry," Dante says, "I'll guide you." He stops and leads me carefully inside. "Just wait till you see," he tells me, a lilt in his voice.

"See what?" I ask.

"The paintings. Some of the best you can find anywhere."

"How can I see anything? It's so dark."

"Just wait." His voice is eager.

He leads me forward; It's dark and I can't see much, but I can smell the earth and the rocks all around me. Dante seems to know his way very well. His stride is sure and confident. We make a turn, and suddenly it's light. I look up to see a round opening at the top. Then I see the paintings—dancing men and women, animals, suns, stars, plants and hunting men wearing animal disguises.

"These are all from prehistoric times?" I ask, amazed.

"Yes, among the oldest ever found on earth."

"Wow! The colors are so vivid."

"Aren't they." There is fierce pride in his voice. "They are done in bat guano."

"Do you know how old they are?"

"Our scientists say they're from the early Bronze age. Some believe they may even be older than one in Indonesia that is supposed to be the oldest in the world."

"But why isn't this more of a tourist attraction?" I ask.

"For one thing, my father decided not to broadcast the findings. He didn't want what happened to the Lascaux Caves where the carbon dioxide of the thousands of tourists arriving everyday started to visibly damage the paintings."

I gaze at the paintings in amazement. "How long ago were these caves discovered?"

"I was a child when a rock climber found them, but I still remember the day I heard the news. I was so excited. Even before they were authenticated I was already here with Matilda."

"Really?"

"Look here," he says showing me the footprint of a small child.

"Wow. This is even better than visiting a cemetery. It's hard to imagine that this child lived thousands of years ago and left something of itself for us to find."

"See that guy there with the big penis?"

I follow the direction of his hand. Indeed, there is a man with an extraordinarily large erection. "Yeah?"

"That's how you make me feel."

He grasps my shoulders and draws me toward him. "You thought I was kidding when I said I wanted to get you alone in the caves, didn't you?"

"Well … I must confess I had hoped."

"I've always liked a hopeful girl," he murmurs as his lips descend on mine, warm, fiery and demanding. His scent floods my senses and I lose myself in him. My hands rise up to entwine in the silky hair at the nape of his neck as I press myself against his hard body and kiss him back until the world falls away and I can no longer think straight.

"Rosa," he whispers slowly, as if it is a magic incantation. Never has my name sounded so wonderful before. My heart flutters in my chest.

"What?" I gasp breathlessly.

The moment is shattered by the sound of his cellphone ringing. He pulls his phone out and looks at it. He looks at me and says, "Hold that thought," before taking the call and saying joyfully, "*Oncle*."

"No, I'm sorry, but Rosa has to nap in the afternoon. In her condition, she gets tired too easily." He pauses to listen, his eyes on me. "Are you sure? I don't want to put you out." He pauses again. "All right, great." Another pause. "Of course, we'll be there." Another pause. "No, no.

GEORGIA LE CARRE

Just a snack will do. Okay. We'll see you in …
half-an-hour."

He looks at me. "Can I take a raincheck on ravishing you?
My uncle wants me to bring you around to his house."

"You want me to meet him dressed like this?"

"You won't meet a man less concerned with the way you look
than my uncle."

As we walk back to the car he tells me about the man who
was more a father to him than his own.

CHAPTER 30

Rosa

*D*ante's uncle lives in a large, gated house. The grounds are filled with trees. His uncle and aunt are waiting outside to meet us. To my surprise, he looks like an older version of Dante. In the car, Dante explained that his uncle is actually his mother's brother.

His aunt hugs me warmly before she opens her arms out to Dante. Instead of hugging her, Dante sweeps her off the ground and whirls her around while she screams with laughter and begs him to put her down. I cannot help but smile to see Dante so happy. It is a completely different Dante than the one of last night in the company of his father and stepmother.

By the time he consents to put her down her face is quite red and glowing. She turns to me breathlessly. "Oh, he is a terrible one, my boy."

We are shown to a sunny room where cakes and sandwiches have been set on a table. A maid starts pouring out tea for us and Helen politely asks about me. My job, my life in England, where Dante and I first met. The conversation is easy and pleasant. All the while his uncle smiles and nods and says almost nothing. He waits until we are almost finished eating before he asks the question that has no doubt been burning in his chest.

"Will you become King, Dante?"

Dante frowns. "No, Oncle. I won't. You know how I feel about blood succession. If Father wants he can pick Linnus to be his successor."

His uncle's face hardens. "Your father does not have the right to pick a successor of his choice. You are his successor. It is time for you to stand up and be counted. To take charge. It is your responsibility. You are failing in your duty for your country."

"*Oncle*, you know how I feel about monarchy. If I had my way, this country would be a democracy."

For the first time, Anton shows his frustration. He bangs his fist on the table making the teacups rattle.

"Don't say that. Don't ever say that. Look around you, at all those countries with democratically elected governments. They are nothing but corrupt lackeys of the multinational corporations. Do the people in those countries have more than us?" he bellows.

"No, they don't," he answers his own question. "Have they more freedom than our people? Do their citizens have more peace than we do? The answer to all those questions is always no. No. No. They do not have a better system than us."

I glance at Dante who is staring at his uncle.

"Are you aware that your father is in the process of signing us to treaties so that soulless international corporations can take our country to international tribunals for arbitration if they feel the decisions our government makes are not in their best interests or hurt their profits? Their rights will be above ours!"

Dante's eyes narrow. "Father is signing Avanti up to T.T.I.P and T.T.P?"

"I think it is your brother who is brokering the deal," his uncle says heavily. "You have to stop the process, Dante. You have to stop the rot. The last great leader was your grandfather, and I believe with all my heart that you can be the next. You must step up. Avanti needs a strong and wise leader. Do your duty. One day your child could hate you for snatching away what is his or her birthright."

He stands up stiffly and starts walking away.

Dante jumps up. "*Oncle*," he calls.

His uncle stops, looks at him sadly, and says, "I have kept my promise to your mother and done everything I can for you. There is no more I can say. Do your duty. Make your mother proud." Then he walks away.

"There are other things afoot too," his aunt whispers. You have to come back. You have to do something to stop Linnus and your father. They're destroying the country so they can buy bigger yachts and more expensive watches and clothes for their wives. Please, Dante," she begs.

*D*ante is very quiet in the car. His face is like stone and I know he is thinking about what his uncle said so I don't try to start a conversation. It seems wrong for me to talk of anything trivial after the momentous revelations in his uncle's house. He escorts me to my room and slides the back of his hand down my cheek.

"Go to sleep, Rosa. Don't tire yourself out too much during your shopping trip."

"I won't," I whisper.

"I'll see you tonight, *bella*," he says with a smile, then he is gone.

I lie on my bed, but I am unable to sleep. I feel as if I have been thrown right in the middle of a maelstrom. I call Star, then Cindy, but neither is around. As I close my eyes, someone knocks on my door.

"Come in," I call, thinking it will be Elsa, but to my shock, the queen enters.

CHAPTER 31

Rosa

*S*he is wearing a cream two-piece Dior. If I remember correctly, she is wearing it with the same shoes the model wore on the catwalk. I scramble out of bed and drop into a small curtsy.

"Ah, I have caught you while you were sleeping," she observes quietly.

"No, not at all. I was just lying down."

"That's good. Will you come with me? I want to show you something."

She turns and starts walking away. I hesitate for an instant then I follow her out of the room. We walk down the corridor into the west wing.

"So ... you and Dante are not staying on?" she asks, glancing at me.

"I don't think so."

"Why not?'

I bite my lip, not sure what I should say. "I think Dante prefers to live in Italy and of course, I have my job too."

"Your job at the magazine?"

"Yes."

"Ah. That is nothing. You can easily find another one or Dante can set you up with a magazine. Surely he must have pulled some strings to get you your job in the first place?"

There is nothing I can say to that because that is true. My spine becomes straighter. "Yes, but he doesn't want to live here."

"Surely, you must have realized by now that a woman can persuade her man to do whatever she wants."

If she was anyone else but Dante's stepmother … I take a deep breath. "I don't want to manipulate Dante to do anything he does not want to do, Your Majesty. I want him to be happy."

She smiles slowly. "How naïve you are, Rosa. Dante's life is not in Italy. It is here, and so is yours."

I stare at her. I don't understand what is going on. I understood why Dante's uncle wanted him to come back, but why does she? We come to a door.

"Look," she says and opens the door. She holds back while I walk into it. I look around it in a daze. It is a nursery. The walls are cream with a gorgeous gold and maroon wallpaper on one wall. There is a gold cot with the coat of arms painted on the side. An antique rocking horse stands under a tall window.

"This will be your baby's nursery. I had it aired and prepared," she says behind me.

I walk to the rocking horse. It has such sad eyes.

"That belonged to Dante," she says softly.

I try to imagine Dante rocking on it in this huge cold room. I touch it and it starts to silently rock. I know without any doubt she is poison. She does not have my best interest at heart. I don't want to live in this palace with her. I don't want my child to sit on this old horse, lie in that gold cot, or have to live in this massive cold room so far away from his parents, always tended by nannies. I turn around to face her. Her eyes are cold and watching.

I smile politely at her. "Thank you for showing me this room. I will certainly think about what you said."

She nods and turns away from me. "Good. It will be wonderful to see children running around in this palace again."

"It is up to Dante," I say softly. I refuse to let her manipulate me into making Dante do something he doesn't believe in.

"Of course." She smiles, but it doesn't reach her eyes. "I understand Cassandra is taking you shopping this afternoon."

"Yes. We're supposed to leave about two."

"That's nice." She rings a bell on the wall.

I look at her awkwardly and she stares back at me. Not saying a word.

Her look makes me want to fidget. "I guess I better be getting back to my room."

"I've rung for the help. Someone will show you back to your chamber."

I wish I could have told her that I knew the way back, but I'm not sure I can find my way back. "Oh, thanks."

The minutes with her with neither of us speaking feel like a lifetime. I almost kiss the short, fat woman who arrives at her bidding.

"Thank you again for showing me this room."

"You're most welcome," she says so expressionlessly it actually leaves me cold.

CHAPTER 32

Rosa

*I*nside my room, I stand gazing blankly out the window. When I came to Avanti I never expected to be in the middle of such strong family politics. I stand watching birds flying by and after a time I spy a man riding on a horse, but it's such a distance from the palace that I'm not sure if it's Dante or not. Still he is a good rider, fast and sure.

I watch him until there is a knock on my door.

"Ready?" Cassandra asks when I open the door.

"Ready," I say with a smile. "Just let me grab my purse."

"You won't need it."

"I won't?"

"Dante wants to pay for everything."

I can't help the surprised expression on my face.

She laughs. "Don't worry. You'll get used to it. Being able to buy whatever you like. Never having to choose between A or B. It's actually a lovely feeling."

"It must be," I say softly.

She laughs. "Come on, let's go."

We settle into the back of a grey Mercedes. The ride into the city is quick as there is almost no traffic. I gaze curiously out of the window at the changing scenery. The thing that strikes me most is how clean and fresh everything looks: the perfect condition of the streets, the sidewalks, and the buildings. There is not so much as a cigarette butt littering the ground. Eventually, the car pulls up at the entrance of a place called Louis Rye Sart.

"This is it," Cassandra says. "My favorite store. Since we don't have much time and we need to get you something for tonight I thought we'll just go here. I'm sure you'll be impressed."

She gets out of the car, and I follow her. There is a CLOSED sign on the door.

"It's closed," I say.

Cassandra laughs. "I know. They closed it for us, silly."

A blonde woman in a stylish suit opens the heavy glass door. "Good afternoon, Your Highness," she says with a bow. She turns to me. "My name is Freja and it is an honor to welcome you to our shop, Miss Winchester."

The store is like an art gallery. The walls and ceiling are white and there are no racks of dresses and blouses or shelves filled with merchandise. Instead, mannequins dressed in the latest Italian and French fashions stand in alcoves and niches throughout the store.

"This way, please," she says, leading us into an elevator.

When the doors open, we enter an area that looks similar to one of the rooms in the palace. This is obviously the special saloon that was reserved for the super-rich. The décor had been chosen to make them feel at home.

"I have something very special for Miss Winchester to wear to the ball. If she likes it we will make all necessary alterations and have it sent to the palace in two hours."

A woman dressed in black comes forth, a dress draped over her outstretched arms. Freja lifts the dress by the hanger's hook and holds it up for me to see.

I work in the fashion industry, but I cannot help the gasp that exits my mouth. When I was young I used to read books about dresses that were made by elves. This dress looks like it has been made by a little child going blind in India. The floor length gown is so meticulously hand-embellished with pearls and tiny crystals that one can hardly see the saffron colored background material.

"It's perfect," Cassandra declares. She turns to me. "You must try it."

Before I know it, I have been herded into a plush changing room and the woman in black is silently helping me into the dress.

Cassandra pushes aside the velvet curtain and clasps her hands. "Why, it doesn't even need to be altered. It is wonderful."

I stare at myself. It is definitely the most beautiful thing I have ever worn, but the kind of work that has gone into it makes it an haute couture gown and I'm not about to blow £30,000 or something equally ridiculous of Dante's money on such a dress. No way. I'd be embarrassed to do something like that.

"It's very beautiful, but how much is it?" I ask.

It is as if I said I was planning to kill someone. Both shop assistants start with surprise and Cassandra gives me a strange look. "We never talk about prices here. The bills are sent directly to the accounting office."

"But my dress is going to be paid for by Dante. I can't make him pay for a dress as expensive as I know this must be."

Cassandra's smooth brow furrows. "Well, he knew I was bringing you here and he was more than happy with it."

"I can't buy this, Cassandra. I just don't feel comfortable spending this kind of money. Especially since it is not even mine."

"Shall I call Dante?"

I shake my head violently. "No. Of course not."

Her head tilts as she stares at me curiously. "Why not?"

"Because then he will think I want him to buy the dress."

"Oh, don't be such a goose. This is not about you. If you are not dressed in the style and manner that is expected of Dante's fiancée you will embarrass the whole family. People will think you are some kind of ugly duckling that we are mistreating."

I get what she is saying, I don't want to let Dante down, but at the same time ... I just can't spend that kind of money on a dress.

With a sigh she takes her phone out of her bag and dials out a number. She speaks rapidly into it in Avantian. She ends the call and smiles at me. "I told you it would be fine. Dante told me to spare no expense." She turns to the two women watching us with round eyes. "Now we need a purse and shoes to match."

The assistants bring purses with no price tags on them. I stare at them in confusion. I can still hear Dante's aunt saying, 'they're destroying the country so that they can buy bigger yachts and more expensive watches and clothes for their wives.' Cassandra picks up a gorgeous one with a pearl clasp.

"You like this? It will be perfect with your dress."

"Yes, it's gorgeous."

"Then let's get it. Now shoes." She turns briskly to the assistant. "Please hurry. We don't have much time."

I choose a pair of lovely silk shoes with crystal heels. They come in a silver box with black satin lining.

"If you see anything else you especially like," Cassandra says with a smile, "don't hesitate."

"No, that is fine," I say quickly. I have never shopped like this before. It is disconcerting to not know how much the items I am buying cost. I think I am actually horrified by the idea.

Cassandra laughs, then leans close to me. "What is that expression in English?" she whispers. "It's just a drop in the bucket. There is far more where this came from."

I turn to face her, surprised by the naked greed in her voice.

"You should see the expression on your face," she teases.

"I'm not from a rich family so I'm just not used to spending money like this."

She laughs gaily. "Trust me, you'll take to it like a duck to water. Right. Let's go. We do have to be back in time for the hair stylists."

I nod. "I'd almost forgotten."

"Can't forget something like that," she says. "After all we want to look our very best."

"Yes, of course," I murmur softly.

She is fun to be with and I'm grateful to her for helping me find a dress that will be considered suitable for Dante's fiancée to wear to a palace ball, but something about her makes me feel uncomfortable.

I am glad that Dante and I will not be living at the palace.

CHAPTER 33

Dante
https://www.youtube.com/watch?v=-Oo_73SlOwk
A quiet angel on the sun
(Un Angelo Disteso Al Sole)

*S*he's always accused me of being a player, and yeah, I was, the King of Seduction himself. All the women were just about pleasure. With her it's so different. This deep longing for the feel of her skin, her taste, her smile.

I'd planned to tell her how I really feel about her, but when I see her standing in her ball gown it feels like I've been sucker-punched. The air leaves me in a gasp. There are no words in my head or on my tongue. Surely this creature can't be a flesh and blood woman. Only an angel could shine like this.

Her brow knits. "Is something wrong?"

I shake my head. Still in a daze.

"I … I … honestly didn't want you to buy this dress for me. I … I … could tell it was too expensive, but Cassandra said that if I didn't wear something like this … it would reflect … um … badly on your family so … I really didn't have a choice. I'm sorry," she stammers.

I stride up to her and put my fingers over her mouth. "I would have gladly paid anything to see you in this dress."

"Oh, do you like it?"

"Fuck the dress. You look incredible."

She blushes. "Thank you. You look pretty hot yourself."

I could have told her then, but there is a noise behind us. I turn and Viggo is standing behind me holding two velvet boxes.

"Her Majesty wanted Miss Winchester to wear these pieces of jewelry to the party," he says with a slight bow.

I take the boxes from him and open the boxes. To my shock the first one is one of my mother's necklaces and the matching bracelet. I can still remember her wearing the necklace one night she came into my room to kiss me good night. The memory is still sharp. I even remember her special perfume. When I put my arms around her neck the clasp scratched me.

I examine the clasp, there is still that rough edge on it. I open the other box and it holds a pearl orchid hairpin. I had never seen my mother wearing it, but I know it is hers. Only she would wear sweet little pieces like this.

I look into Rosa's eyes.

"What's the matter?"

"These belonged to my mother."

She gasps and covers her mouth. "I don't have to wear them, Dante. This dress is already so full of pearls and stones. There is no need for more bling."

"Rosa, Rosa, Rosa. Turn around."

She falls silent and looks up at me with wide eyes.

I press the clasp down with my fingernail, so that it does not cut her soft skin, and carefully fit it around her slender neck. I turn her back to face me and sigh with satisfaction. Nothing has ever felt as right as Rosa wearing my mother's jewelry. Gently, I pin the pearl flower into her hair, and fix the bracelet around her slim wrist.

I take her to a mirror and let her look at herself.

"We make a lovely couple, don't we?" she whispers.

I will tell her tonight when we come back here. I will tell her while we are in bed. Now I am too overwhelmed by her in this dress, by my mother's jewelry, and by the decision I have taken. A decision that will change the trajectory of both our lives.

CHAPTER 34

Rosa

By the time Dante and I reach the curtained entrance of the vast ballroom, the floor is already crowded. Everything is picture perfect. The chandeliers are sparkling, an orchestra is playing, all the men are in tuxedos, and the women are in designer gowns and dripping with jewels.

A man in a maroon suit announces us, "Prince Nils Dante de-Beauvouli and his fiancée, Miss Rosa Winchester."

Everybody in the room turns to look at us as we go down the marble steps. It feels unreal, almost like the way it is in movies. Dante nods to several men, and I try to keep my smile polite and confident as we walk up to where his father and stepmother are standing with Linnus and Cassandra. They are flanked by fawning Court courtiers. Linnea is wearing a blood-red gown that makes her stand out amongst all the other women around her.

We pay our respects to them. For a second Dante's father

stares at me as if he does not recognize me, then he smiles distantly. Linnea's eyes dip down to my necklace before she smiles serenely at me.

"You look wonderful, my dear."

"Doesn't she just," Cassandra says.

"Yes, she's quite the beauty," Linnus remarks softly.

I feel myself blush.

Dante turns to me. "Shall we?"

"Yes," I say with relief.

We join the whirlwind of moving feet and flaring skirts. This is the first time Dante has taken me in his arms on the dance floor, but it feels just right. I can tell immediately that he's an excellent dancer, and easier to follow than anyone I've danced with.

"Do you realize everyone is watching us?" I ask sotto voce.

"Imagine them all sitting on toilets."

I almost grin. "I can't go around imagining everybody sitting on toilets."

"I don't see why not. Most of the time they sound like they're spewing shit anyway."

This time I break into a giggle.

As Dante sweeps me around I see the queen and king dancing. Linnea is smiling and so is the king. It is almost impossible to believe they are the same oddly matched couple from last night.

To my surprise, I see Linnus heading toward us. He taps Dante's shoulder.

"May I?"

Dante steps back, a tight smile on his face. "Of course."

Linnus takes me in his arms. He's a good dancer, but there is something about him that makes me feel wary. Unlike Dante who is cocky, but genuine, this man is arrogant and up his own ass. Intuition also tells me he doesn't like me.

"Enjoying your stay at the palace?" he asks, his eyes full of deception.

"Very much, thank you."

"Avanti is nice when you don't have to live here."

My skin starts to crawl. If we were anywhere else, and he was anyone else but Dante's younger brother, I would have stopped the dance and walked away. But, I'm the center of attraction and the last thing I need is to make a scene. I smile sweetly. "Since we don't plan to live here there should be no problem."

He doesn't smile back. "Wonderful."

That is the extent of the conversation as we swirl through the room to a Strauss waltz. As soon as the music stops, Dante is back to claim me.

"You look like you imagined him sitting on a toilet," he says.

All the tension in my body flows out and I nearly break out in laughter. "You do know your brother is a prick, don't you?"

"Trust me, it was harder for me to watch him dancing with you than it was for you to dance with him."

I look into his beautiful eyes. "You're not jealous?"

"I wanted to knock his stupid head off for touching you."

"You brother doesn't want to sleep with me. He actually doesn't even like me."

"Then, you don't understand human beings at all. My brother would sleep with you in a heartbeat. It would mean he was taking something that belonged to me."

"Dante, why did you bring me to meet your family when there is no love lost between you and them?"

"Because I want to marry you and I had to follow certain procedures, Rosa. I'm proud of you and I want everyone to know that I have found the woman I want to spend the rest of my life with. But I have to admit, I didn't expect to walk into this shit storm with my uncle or what is happening here. A lot has changed in the last two years. None of it for the better."

The music stops and Dante leads me to the sidelines. He snags two champagne flutes and orders a glass of orange juice for me. He hands me one of the glasses.

"To us," he says lifting his glass.

"To us," I echo and take a tiny sip.

"If I may be so bold?" a voice asks from our left.

We both turn to see Dante's father standing a foot away. We were both so engrossed in each other we had not even noticed his arrival.

I hand my glass to Dante. "Of course."

He smiles faintly. "Let the master show you how it's done."

"Ah, yes, but which one of us is the master?" Dante remarks, a strange smile on his face.

"We'll soon see, won't we?" the king says, putting one arm around my waist and holding my hand with the other. Maybe he is the master, I decide, after a few steps.

"You certainly know the moves, Your Majesty," I say.

"I should." He laughs. "I've been practicing for a long, long time."

"Well, it shows." Through the corner of my eye I can see the queen. She is talking to someone, but she is keeping a watchful eye on us.

"You will be leaving tomorrow?" he asks.

"Yes."

"That's good."

I look into his eyes as he swirls me around. "Why is it good?"

His steps never falter. "Because a bird's place is in the sky and the rooftops, not in the burrows the fox has built for its own family."

I feel goosebumps rise up on my arms. "Is that why you sent your son away to live in with his uncle?"

"It seems we understand each other perfectly."

"Don't worry. Neither Dante nor I want to live in this palace."

A strange expression flickers across his face. It is almost like pain. "It would seem my son has chosen wisely."

After that there is no more to say and we dance in silence. When the music stops, he looks me directly in the eyes and presses a key into my hand. It is warm from his skin. "Here. This is my life's work. It is the only thing I have done that I am truly proud of. Ask my son to show you."

"What is it?"

"The South Garden. It's prettiest in spring when my apple trees look like shadowy claws, but it is still quite something now."

As he steps back, nods formally, and turns away, I stare after him as Dante comes up to me. "You look quite surprised. What on earth did he say to you?"

"Will you take me to see the South Garden, Dante?"

"The South Garden? No one except my father goes there, and it is locked away at all times. I'll ask my father for the key tomorrow and show it to you then."

I open my palm. "Your father gave me the key."

His eyebrows rise with astonishment. "He did?"

I nod. "He wanted me to ask you to show me around the garden. He said it was the only thing he has done that he is proud of."

Dante's head jerks back. "He told you *that*?"

"Yes. Why are you so surprised?"

"Well, as far as I know, my father never allows anyone to go into his garden. He keeps the only key to it. When I went to see him the other day, he was waiting for me close to the entrance and as soon as he saw me, he came out and we had a drink together in the conservatory."

"Wow." I turn around and see his father talking to a man. His posture is stiff and distant as he listens to whatever the man is saying.

"Let's go see his garden then." Dante steers me past the dancing couples and out a double door at the end of the ballroom.

The night is perfect, a cool breeze is blowing, and the sky is filled with stars. We walk on a stone-flagged path past the formal gardens. At the edge of the maze Dante lifts some creepers and fits the key into a secret door.

"Oh, my God. How exciting. Your father has a secret garden."

"Yes, he has always had it. It was actually started by my great-grandmother who lived to be 102. When she died, my grand-mother had neither the interest nor the ability, so my father took over. He was sixteen then and he has been tending to this garden all his life. I still remember following him around when I was a child. The sound of spring to me was not pigeons cooing it was the sound of shears. My father's shears busy in the garden."

He pushes open the door.

Even before he goes to a metal box and switches on the lights I see how enchanted and fey the garden seems to be. It has a magical quality that I haven't seen anywhere else. There are midges hanging like pixie dust in the air. The smell of spearmint wafts in the gentle wind, and an owl hoots in the dark like a soul lost in the darkness. Here and there delicate marble statues half-hidden in foliage glint under the moonlight.

Once he hits the switch, my jaw drops.

CHAPTER 35

Rosa
https://www.youtube.com/watch?v=AfXR-EZG9s8
Touch My Soul

*T*he full splendor is revealed. Within the tall hedges the place is lighted only by fairy lights, which makes it almost seem to be under a spell. As we follow the winding path deeper into that unearthly garden, there are full-throated white flowers, lipstick-pink peonies, and ponds where frog spawn glistens like precious diamonds. There are no formal geometric patterns here. Only a profusion of nature growing in every available space. When I touch the leggy flowers, I feel electricity rush through me.

Dante leads me further in and I spy more flowers. Our presence startles a dozy hedgehog that scuttles into some bushes. Right in the middle of the garden, a fountain spouts water into the air. Iridescent fish swim in the water.

"Your father has created his own truly beautiful world here. No wonder he does not allow anyone to disturb it. They simply wouldn't understand. This is heaven on earth."

"Why do you think he gave you the key?"

I search Dante's face. "I don't know."

"I think he knew you belonged here. This garden needs a goddess."

"What do you mean?"

"Strip for me, Rosa?"

"Are you serious?"

"I've never been more serious," he says huskily. In the dark, his eyes glitter, making my heart ache with love.

"We can't have sex here, Dante. It'll be almost sacrilege."

"How wrong you are, *bella*. It will be beautiful."

"But—"

"Trust me."

"What if someone comes in?" I whisper.

"I locked the door."

I bite my bottom lip uncertainly.

"I need to see you naked in this garden, Rosa. I need to taste you."

He steps away from me and waits. I ease down the zip of my dress, and it falls on the springy grass. I step out of it and remove my strapless bra, and then I slide my panties down my legs. I stand in front of him, nude but for the necklace and bracelet. I see his chest rise and fall as he breathes. He takes his jacket off and lays it on the ground behind me.

"Lie down," he says huskily.

I obey. The inside of the jacket is still warm from his body. The grass tickles the backs of my legs. I smell the earth and the smell of things growing in the dark. It smells like baked apples. He stands over and looks down at me. His gaze is possessive and full of fierce pride.

"Spread your legs, *bella*."

I push my legs up and let them butterfly on either side. Wide open, I gaze up at him.

"You cannot imagine what you look like," he whispers as he kneels down. His mouth finds a nipple. He sucks it and my body arches with pleasure. He slides a finger into me. I'm so wet his finger makes a squishing sound. He adds another finger and I moan. I feel drunk with pleasure and I want more and more.

Slowly, he kisses and licks his way down my body until his tongue can reach out and lick my slit. Then his tongue goes to work. He laps at my folds and circles my clit. His other hand pushes back my hood and his lips capture the hard bud.

My hands clench in his hair as I gaze up at the vast sky, the stars. I rock back and forth against his face mindlessly. Thrusting my pussy harder and harder into his face and mouth. I want to remember this until the day I die.

I don't want to come so quickly.

I want this to last and last, but his tongue flicks back and forth so fast and furiously, I can hold back no longer. My body starts trembling. As I crest, he bites down on my clit, making me scream into the night. My body jerks and my thighs crush his head.

I feel myself filling his mouth with my liquid while he keeps pumping his fingers right through my extended orgasm. When it is all over, he rams his tongue one last time into me.

Then he brings his mouth to mine and plunges his tongue into my mouth. His tongue tastes of me. I suck it desperately. I feel as if I need him in my mouth more than I need to breathe. Our mouths meld in a sensation of heat. Oh God, I love this man so much I don't know where he begins and I end. Eventually, he lifts his head and looks down at me.

"Fuck, baby. You're so fucking beautiful."

I want to say the words. It seems like the perfect place to tell him I love him. All I have to say is I love you so much, but my throat locks, and I don't say anything, I just stare up into his beautiful face.

He unzips his pants quickly, and pulls them down his hips. He pushes his underpants down and his cock springs out, hard and almost purple in the moonlight.

"You belong only to me. This is the only cock that you will ever have in your body again," he says as he pushes slowly into me, his eyes dark and hooded.

After all this time, I still have to get used to his size, to the sensation of being so stretched and full. He stops to allow me to adjust then he grinds his hips against my pussy. I'm so soaked and I can hear the sticky sounds of his skin against mine.

"My need is too strong, *bella*. I can't last," he mutters thickly.

He must have been really holding himself back, because in a few thrusts, his whole body clenches, and with a roar he fills me with his seed. I know he likes to stay for a while inside my body after he has come so I gently stroke his face. Eventually, he moves, molds his body to mine.

"Told you it would be beautiful," he murmurs.

"Yes, it was." One day I'll tell him how beautiful it really was for me. How it felt as if I was making love amongst the stars.

"Almost perfection, isn't it?" he asks.

"I'm not sure about the almost part," I say. "I'm pretty convinced this night is totally perfect."

I tell him I'd felt some trepidation about the ball. I'd never been to one before, but now I wouldn't have missed it for the world.

Once more we kiss, and I cling to him as if I never want to let him go. I don't want to leave this enchanted garden and go back to the real world.

"Ready to go back to the party?" he asks when we break apart.

"I suppose we should."

He helps pull my zip up for me. Some bits of my hair have escaped the pins, so I pull everything out, and let my hair loose.

"Here, keep this," I say dropping the pearl pins that belonged to his mother into his trouser pocket.

As we walk back to the party, my shoes start to hurt my feet. I tell Dante I'm going to go up to my room to change my shoes. He offers to come up with me, but I tell him I'll meet him at the entrance of the ballroom. When I reach the lobby, I see Cassandra hurrying up to me.

"Where have you been?" she asks, her eyes roaming knowingly over my hair.

I don't know why, but I don't want to tell her that I've been in the South Garden. "We just went for a walk," I tell her.

"A walk?" She smirks. "That's a new name for it."

I shrug and smile.

"Aren't you going back to the party?"

"Yes, but I'm going to change my shoes first. These shoes are killing me."

"Well, what a coincidence because I was just about to go up and change my shoes too." She lifts her lime green dress and shows me her sparkly shoes.

"I saw you dancing with Linnus's father," she says as we walk side by side up the winding staircase with a huge crystal chandelier hanging over us.

"Yes, I had no idea he is such a wonderful dancer," I say mildly.

"The two of you looked marvelous waltzing around the dance floor. I think he likes you. A lot."

"That's kind of you to say, but considering the stern looks he throws my way, I didn't really think he approved of me at all."

"He gave you something, didn't he?"

I don't look at her and I keep my voice casual. "Yeah, he gave me the key to the South Garden. He wanted Dante to show it to me."

"So that's where you were. Why didn't you just tell me that instead of pretending you went for a walk?"

I turn to face her. She is staring at me with a hurt expression. "I didn't tell you because it's not important, Cassandra. He thought I would like to see it because I like gardens, but there is nothing to it."

"If it's not that important why hide it?"

"Look, I'm sorry I didn't tell you. It was just a private memory between Dante and me and I wanted to keep it that way. Do you understand where I'm coming from?"

She laughs. "I was just yanking your leg. Of course, I understand. I knew you and Dante had been having it off somewhere."

I smile with relief. For a moment there, I thought I had just made another enemy in the palace. The sooner I get out of here, the better. As we walk up, I can't help but glance up at the chandelier.

"This palace is so beautiful—"

The words are cut off when I feel Cassandra's foot slip off the next step and kick hard against my left leg. To my horror, it causes me to lose my balance. My arms flail and I turn towards her hoping to catch hold of her, but she makes a quick, nimble movement away from me. I try to grab the banister, but it is outside my reach.

In a moment frozen in time I see Cassandra turn to look at me, a wicked smile flashing across her face. It's there for only a second, then it disappears as quickly as it appeared. As my body hits the hard marble stairs, I see a schooled look of concern displace that triumphant smile.

A sharp pain radiates in my side.

Then I am rolling like a bowling ball down the stairs, bouncing, my body hitting every hard edge. I hear a roar of disbelief from somewhere in the vast lobby as I continue to tumble down the steps. I know it is Dante shouting for me. I land on my back with a thud, and lie there, with my legs askew, like a rag doll. For a moment or two I can't move. I'm too stunned and shocked.

Then Dante's face is hovering above me. I think he is talking to me because his mouth is moving, but I can't make out what he is saying. I am in a fog. I recognize the terrible distress on his handsome face through a haze of pain.

And I see her. The woman who deliberately caused my fall. She is crying. Other people start rushing towards us.

CHAPTER 36

Dante
https://www.youtube.com/watch?v=4T4EB3dl9j8
Russian Roulette

I watch Rosa and Cassandra ascend the stairs together. I cannot imagine a life without her or our child. Already the baby, yet unborn, has changed my life.

What happens next plays out in slow motion. I will see it in my mind's eye forever. I see her reach out to Cassandra to catch her balance, and Cassandra steps out of the way. She doesn't scream.

She simply falls.

Oh Jesus!

I start sprinting towards her, as if I can catch her mid-fall. I don't. I feel every jarring hit she takes inside me. She lands on the ground and doesn't move. My heart stops beating. I've never been more terrified in my life as I reach her and look down. Her eyes are open as I kneel beside her.

I jerk my phone out of my pocket. I dial the three-digit emergency number reserved for the royal family and the moment I hear a voice, I say with as much authority as I can muster, "This is Prince Nils de-Beauvouli. There has been an accident in the palace ballroom. Send an ambulance immediately." I drop the phone.

"Everything is going to be fine. I've called an ambulance already. It will be here in a moment."

"The baby," Rosa gasps, her blue eyes filled with fear.

I lean over and kiss her on the cheek. "He will be fine. The little prince is tough!"

"Or little princess," she mumbles, her eyes closing.

"Don't close your eyes. Stay with me," I say urgently as I reach down and grab her hand. It feels clammy. I squeeze it lightly.

"Something is wrong. It's not just the pain from the bruises. My baby. I want to try to sit up," she says.

"No, no, you can't. You have to remain still until the medics arrive." I glance away. "They're coming." I see them entering the ballroom from the back door. They are usually stationed very close by during functions.

"I feel dizzy. Don't leave me," she says, her voice sounding frightened.

"No, I'll be right here, and I'll ride with you in the ambulance. I'm not going to leave your side for a second."

"My baby," she cries faintly. Then her eyes fall shut and her hand slips out of mine.

I am aware of a large, muscular man in a white EM uniform coming towards us. "I think she's fainted," I cry out in a panic.

"Please step aside, Your Highness," he says. "Only for a moment. We have to hook her up to our monitors."

I step back and he and his companion squat down beside Rosa. He shines a pen light into her eyes.

She must have come around again, because she moans in distress.

They attach their machines to her, then the burly EM starts asking her questions.

At that moment Cassandra touches my shoulder, her face is red and tear streaked. "I'm so sorry. I couldn't do anything."

"How did it happen?" I ask her, my gut burning with hatred.

"It was an accident. I slipped on a step, and my foot hit Rosa's leg. I guess it knocked her off balance. I am so sorry. God, it's awful. I wish I had fallen instead of Rosa."

"Yes, I wish it had been you too," I snarl.

Cassandra looks shocked to hear the raw hate spewing out of me. "How dare you?" she gasps.

My father appears in front of me. "Not here," he says warningly.

Linnus pushes my father out of the way. "Apologize to my wife right now."

"Fuck you." I push my face close to his self-satisfied, smug face. "I saw what happened. Your wife deliberately tripped my fiancée and caused her to fall."

"Dante," Rosa calls out weakly.

"This is not over," I say coldly, before turning away and going back to kneel next to Rosa. "I'm here. I'm right here beside you," I say softly. Then I stand back a little so that she can see me, but I am not in the way of the EMs. The burly EM asks her how many fingers he is holding up. She gets the answer right.

While the second EM continues to work on Rosa, the other one turns to me. "No broken bones, but she might have a concussion. We won't know until the doctors run some tests on her at the hospital."

"She's pregnant," I say, and my voice sounds hoarse and broken.

He frowns. "Right." He addresses his colleague. "Let's go. We need to get her into the hospital as quickly as possible."

I move back to Rosa. "They are going to put you on a gurney. I'm going to move and let them do their work, but I'll be right here beside you."

She groans in pain and I have to clench my hands to stop from punching something or someone. My heart hurts seeing her being lifted on the gurney. As the EM's roll her across the lobby, people are crowded around the edges staring at her.

The ride in the ambulance is a nightmare of watching Rosa slip in an out of consciousness. I hold her hand and I pray, God, how I pray. That she and the baby will be all right. I haven't been to church for years, and I'm afraid that my prayers will go unanswered, but I grasp her hand and I pray.

And I pray.

And I pray.

I close my eyes and I don't see her pale and frightened. I don't hear the siren of the ambulance. I just see her in the moonlight. Naked: a proud, glorious goddess. Don't let her get hurt. Please. Don't let her lose our baby.

"Dante," she moans.

"Shhh ... everything is going to be fine."

I rush along as they push her down the long corridor to a room full of doctors and nurses. I want to enter, but they won't let me follow her inside.

"She's pregnant. Will you make sure she is all right?" I tell an older man in a surgeon's blue smock.

"Your Majesty, please don't worry. I assure you that we will do everything possible to see that both are fine. Please take a seat in the waiting room. I will be out as soon as I know anything."

I almost refuse. I don't want to leave her, and I'm not used to being given orders, not here in Avanti, but reason dictates that I listen to him.

I retreat to the waiting room. It has blue seats that are uncomfortable and a television that is blasting away with some ridiculous game show. Luckily, I am alone. My heart feels so heavy. I pace the floor until the door opens.

"Prince Nils."

I turn to find the gray-haired doctor standing in front of me.

"How is she?"

"She has a slight concussion, but she'll be fine. However, I'm going to keep her in the hospital for a couple of days."

"The baby? What about the baby?"

"The future king is safe."

The breath I was holding rushes out of me. "Has Rosa been told?"

"No, she is just coming around from the sedative we administrated."

"May I see her?"

"Yes." He smiles. "It would actually help if you are there when she wakes up."

I follow the doctor down the hall. He stops in front of a room. "I'll give you some privacy. If you need a nurse, just press the red button on the side of her bed, and one will come immediately." I nod, but I'm barely listening.

I push open the door. My heart hammers when I see her lying on the hospital bed. She looks so small and innocent, almost like a child. I can hardly believe that a couple of hours ago she was lying on my jacket naked and full of life.

I pull the single chair over to her bed and sit down. Gently, I stroke her hand. I turn it over and stroke the soft skin of her wrist. The emotional impact of watching her fall and thinking she could have broken her neck rips into me like a gut punch. I take a deep breath, but I cannot stop the tide of emotion. I bow my head and tears begin to run down my cheeks. I can't stop myself from sobbing quietly. It was such a shock. Such a shock. I thought I'd lost her. Lost our baby.

"Dante."

I glance up, my sobs choking in my chest. She is awake. Her eyes are open. She is trying to talk, but she must be disorientated by the drugs.

"I … I'm okay," she finally manages to say.

"I know. I know," I sob. Standing up, I lean over her and lay my cheek against hers. My voice sounds thick and awful. "The doctor just told me that you are going to be," I squeeze her hand, "be just fine."

CHAPTER 37

Rosa

"So why are you crying ..." I ask. Then it hits me and my body jerks upwards. Pain ratchets all around my body, but I don't care, the words fly out of me like rapid-fire bullets. "Our baby! Is our baby, okay? Is it, Dante? Tell me the truth."

He puts his palms on my cheeks. "Yes, yes, the baby is fine. Calm down."

"Promise?"

He smiles through his tears. "I promise."

I fall back on the pillows tiredly, the last bit of my strength stripped away by that sudden burst of fear.

I take a gasping breath. "So why are you crying?"

"They are tears of happiness, *bella*. They are tears of happiness," he whispers.

Strangely, I recall the look of triumph on Cassandra's face

when she tripped me. "Cassandra … she deliberately tripped me."

"I know she did," he growls, his eyes glowing with hate.

My brain feels foggy. I can't think straight. "I don't know what happened. We were getting along so well. Is it because your father gave me the key? I didn't ask for it. What did I do wrong? She was annoyed I didn't tell her we were in the garden, but surely that is no reason to push me down the stairs."

"No," he says shaking his head. "It's nothing you did. It's my fault."

"Your fault?" I say, shaking my head. My thought process seems to be slow and unfocused. Like there are cobwebs in my brain making everything unclear. Must be the drugs they've given me. My body doesn't take kindly to painkillers. They disorientate me and make me to behave in ways that I wouldn't usually. Once, before I knew what effect they had on me, I almost ruined my entire career by attending a meeting with my bosses while on them.

"How is it your fault? I don't understand."

"By denouncing the throne, I set in motion a plot that will affect any child I have."

"What?"

"Please, Rosa, just hear me out."

"All right, tell me."

"If I don't take the throne after my father, then the rules of ascension state that the first child born of the next generation becomes the rightful heir to the throne."

Seeing that I am about to speak, Dante holds up his hand again. "Cassandra hoped to give birth to the first child, but when I returned with you and announced that you were already pregnant, she saw her dream of giving birth to the future king, or queen of Avanti, die."

My muddled brain struggled with that information. "Oh my God! What a fake bitch. She pretended to be my friend. All that kissing and hugging," I shake my head, "and the whole time she was planning to kill my baby!"

"Yes."

I frown at Dante. "Why did you bring me here knowing that neither I nor our child would be welcome?"

"Rosa, you know I never wanted to be King and I never wanted my child to have the responsibility and pressure of being the next King or Queen either. Because I always made my position clear I thought I was out of their political games and shenanigans. I brought you here for the weekend to make it clear I had found my soul mate, the one I wanted to spend the rest of my life with, and to tell them that I would never be coming back as King. I did not account for how power hungry they have all become. Maybe they were always that greedy. I just didn't know it because I always did my own thing and stayed away from them."

"Hmm … I guess your innocent weekend scared the shit out of them: the useless playboy prince who they had completely written off returns with a woman who is already pregnant with the future ruler of Avanti."

"Yes," Dante admits, his eyes dark and stormy. "I didn't see it coming."

"Oh, Dante." I lift my hand to his face. "It was not your fault. You are not like them. There is not one bad bone in your body, so you couldn't have known what they were capable of."

His face hardens. "Rosa, the blood that runs in their veins runs in mine too. My happiness made me careless, and I underestimated their greed and jealousy. I won't make that mistake again. They are no longer dealing with the playboy prince as they are all going to quickly learn. What was done can be undone!"

"What are you going to do?"

"I need your blessing for what I have to do, Rosa. Avanti might seem like a tiny insignificant country to you, but we are sitting on one of the largest deposits of money in the world! What Linnus is planning will destroy this country and I cannot allow it. It is time for me to step up and be counted."

My heart swells with pride to see Dante grow right before my eyes from a pleasure-seeking player to a real man of strength and a purpose higher than him. Tears fill my eyes. "You don't need my blessing to take back what is your birthright, my darling."

"I do need your blessing, Rosa. You will be my wife. It is important that you understand what you are signing up for. Your whole life is about to change into something unrecognizable. You will have to live in Avanti. You might be able to run your own magazine, but you will most probably be too busy with charitable work to do so. Being royalty is a burden. It's not as glamorous a role in real life as it is in movies. It's a life with little personal freedom. Almost everything is dictated by tradition and rules and expectations, especially expectations. And your every word and action will be examined under a magnifying glass and more often than not criticized."

"My place is next to you, wherever you are."

"Are you sure, because I will abandon my plans in an instant if it will make you unhappy?"

I shake my head. "I'm proud of you, that you have chosen this noble path. Whatever comes our way, we will work it out together. I'm here for the long haul," I say softly.

His shoulders sag with relief, then he straightens them. "I have to go and face the King now. Will you be okay here?"

I smile at him tenderly. "I'm in a hospital. Of course, I'll be fine. Go do what you have to."

He kisses me lingeringly. "Rest. I'll be back soon. I have something important to tell you."

I grin. "Can't wait."

CHAPTER 38

Rosa
https://www.youtube.com/watch?v=ggrz8mzy-e0
It's Not Goodbye.

*A*fter Dante leaves I look around me. There is a remote by the side of the bed. The button to call the nurse is clear. It's red. I press one of the other buttons and the TV comes on. I switch it off and press another. The blinds open.

It is already daylight outside.

I lie back and stare at the lightening sky and think of my baby. My body still feels sore and my head still feels strange as if it doesn't really belong to me, but what a lucky escape the baby and I have had. I think of Dante crying with happiness and a warm feeling fills my chest. We will be fine. Everything will be fine.

A light knock on the door brings me out of my daydream.

"Come in," I call.

Linnea opens the door and immediately my entire body

contracts with fear. My hand reaches for the remote. I hold it in my hand, ready to call the nurse, but I know I am not really in physical danger from her. She is the Queen of Avanti. All the staff would have recognized her as she came into the ward. She won't try anything in a hospital.

"What do you want?" I ask.

"I wanted to make sure you were all right," she says, closing the door.

I look at her incredulously. "Spare me."

"There is no one to blame. You were drinking. It was an accident."

"I did not drink, and it was not an accident," I fume.

"I saw you drinking."

"I took one sip of champagne. I was perfectly sober. I know exactly what happened. Cassandra tripped me deliberately."

She moves her hand distractedly. "She is a silly girl."

"Silly girl?"

"I didn't come here to fight with you, Rosa. Contrary to what you think, I am not your enemy. I came here to warn you. Dante is a nice guy, maybe too nice. He doesn't understand what he has blundered into. Important treaties and agreements are being drawn up and there are billions of dollars at stake. There are people who will kill for a lot less. Avanti is not safe for you, your baby, or Dante anymore. He will never be able to protect his family twenty-four hours a day. Unless you all become prisoners in the palace. And even then, how can he be sure someone will not bribe the servants to poison your child?"

She takes a step closer to me and I feel myself unconsciously shrink back against my pillow.

"Your child will never be safe. Never have a normal life. At any time you could get the dreaded news that the child is dead. It will be an accident, of course. No one will be responsible. The whole world will become hostile. You will never be able to trust anyone again. Just like you mistook Cassandra for your ally. Any person who comes into your life could be the one who will take away the most precious thing you have. Even while you are here, a nurse could come in and inject you with something that will cause you to miscarry. There is no happy ending for you in Avanti, Rosa."

A shiver of fear goes through me. Instinctively, my hands go to cover my belly.

"How will Dante fight this level of evil? It is not just Cassandra, Linnus, and my weak husband he will have to watch. It is all the grasping, deceitful courtiers about whom Dante knows nothing."

I take a deep breath. "I assume you have a solution for me."

"Nobody wants to see you, your baby, or Dante get hurt. Just get out of the way."

My head starts to hurt. "Get out of the way?"

"Take your man and go back to where you came from. You can have a nice life with the man you love and your gorgeous children. You will have more money than you know what to do with, but you have to go now."

"I need to speak to Dante first."

"Please trust me. You know I have no love for you, but I don't wish you harm. And harm will befall you if you remain. As I said before, while you are here, you are vulnerable. Leave. Protect your baby. If you leave Dante will follow. If you stay, he will try to fight them, and it will cause only harm."

I frown.

"Until last night," she continues, "Dante was a player. All he did was party and chase women. He has no experience in politics and he doesn't understand his enemy, so he can never fight them and win. You must believe me. Even if I am being too dramatic, it is better for you to leave than to stay and take the risk that I am wrong. You have nothing to lose by leaving and everything to lose by staying."

I don't feel like my usual self. I feel bewildered and anxious. So many things have happened to me in the last twenty-four hours. There are painkilling drugs rushing around my system. I'm disorientated by my physical injuries. I'm still in shock at Cassandra's betrayal and thinking I lost my baby, and now I'm really frightened for my helpless baby. I feel light-headed and woozy, but what she said does seem to make sense. Dante is a newbie at this and they seem ferocious in their intent to keep the power base. I could stay and fight if I did not have my baby. As it is I have only one duty. To put my unborn child above my own needs. Above all else.

"One of the royal jets is ready to fly you back to England."

I start to feel nauseous and I don't have my dry biscuits. "I need to call Dante and just tell him I'm going."

She shakes her head. "This is exactly what I mean. If you do that you will tip everyone off. You have to slip away. Call him once you are safely out of the country. It is only while you are on Avantian soil that you are in danger."

Everything seems to be moving too quickly for me to comprehend. "My passport. I don't have my passport," I mutter.

"I've got it here. Everything is ready for you."

I run my fingers through my hair. "But I have no clothes."

"I brought Elsa with me. She has packed your suitcase and brought you something to wear. She will fly with you to England and make sure that you arrive safely. Once you arrive, a car will be waiting to take you wherever you want."

She walks to the door, opens it and calls Elsa in.

In a daze, I allow myself to be helped out of bed and into my clothes. Elsa brushes my hair, which has the effect of making me feel even more helpless. Every time I move, pain shoots through my body.

"Do you want more painkillers?" Linnea asks.

"No. That would be bad for the baby," I mumble.

A nurse brings a wheelchair. I sit in it and Elsa pushes me out of the ward, and into the elevator. No one utters a word as we travel downwards.

Once we get out of the doors I see a limousine and outrider escorts waiting for us. The driver holds open the back door. Painfully, I limp into the seat. The door closes, and I wait while Elsa gets in the front passenger seat. The driver gives the signal and the outriders kick off the journey. The car starts to move. I turn and watch Linnea.

There is no expression at all on her smooth face.

Up ahead, all the other cars are making way for us. I was enthralled at having the limo and outriders when we were taken to the palace upon our arrival in Avanti. Now I wish I was on the back of Dante's Vespa.

Those days are gone forever.

That thought is like a knife thrust into my heart. I turn my face to the window and tears fill my eyes. The limo stops on the landing tarmac. The plane with the royal family's crest is waiting. The captain and an air stewardess are standing next to it.

The driver jumps out and opens my door. I get out of the car with great difficulty. Elsa comes to help me walk to the plane.

My hand touches the cold steel railing of the steps. Suddenly, I am homesick. Homesick for my mother. Homesick for Star. Homesick for simple, real people who don't play games with every word they utter.

I put my foot on the first step.

Yes, I'm running away, but I am making the right decision. I'm going back to England where I belong. Where some of this incredible stress will abate. Where my baby will be safe. I'll call Dante when I get there. I'm a strong person. I'll recover from this temporary setback.

Everything will work out.

CHAPTER 39

Dante

*M*y father's butler is standing outside the library, so I know he is inside having a glass of cognac. It's a long tradition for him to retire to his library for cognac and a Cuban cigar. I nod to the old man as he opens the door for me. The disagreeable scent of the cigar slaps me in the face.

My father looks up from the paper he is reading and our eyes meet.

"So the cub comes into the lion's den," my father says.

"No, the lion tamer visits the aging, toothless lion."

"I am as strong as I ever was," he boasts hollowly.

"Then why does your hand tremble?"

His brow creases.

"You think I didn't notice that at the dinner table. You taught me to always closely observe my opponents," I say eyeing his right hand.

"So I am your opponent now?"

"Weren't you always, *Father*?"

The emphasis on the word father is not lost on him. He flinches. "No. Never."

I nod toward his right hand. "Parkinson's?"

For a moment, he looks as though he isn't going to answer. "Early stages," he admits with a sigh.

"You will have to abdicate when it progresses."

"It will be many years before that happens. There are medications to keep it under control. Why do you care? You've renounced the throne."

I smile. "Not officially. Only verbally to you."

He cocks his head. "What does that mean?"

"It means I am the rightful heir to the throne, and I plan on becoming the king when your disease gets so bad you'll be forced to abdicate."

"I could fight you," he says feebly.

I smile. "You won't. You wouldn't want to air the royal dirty laundry."

"We have none," he snaps.

"Your daughter-in-law deliberately injured my fiancée in an effort to make her miscarry so that when she gets herself pregnant her child will become the heir to the throne," I accuse.

My father sags in his seat. He starts to speak, but stops, shakes his head, then tries again. "If that's true, whose fault is it? You told me you didn't want the throne and stormed out. Then you stayed away from Avanti for two years. If you hadn't done that, the conflict of who's child is going to become king wouldn't have arisen."

"Are you excusing her criminal behavior? She wanted to kill your grandson! Doesn't that concern you?"

He pauses like he's in deep thought. "How can you be sure it was not an accident, Dante?"

"I saw it with my own eyes," I roar furiously.

"You can't prove it though."

"No, but the fact is she did, and I can see it in your eyes that you know she did," I say sternly.

"I knew she was ambitious, but I didn't see this coming," he mutters.

I point my finger at my father. "She and my brother are going to pay for this. You are going to ban them from the palace. You will order them to move to the summer cottage by the lake."

He drops his face into his hands. "I can't do that to Linnea's son. It will kill her."

"But, Father, I am going to be king soon. If you don't banish them from the palace, I will exile my brother and Cassandra from Avanti with a pension barely large enough to buy milk and groceries. Would you rather I do that to your favorite son, Father?"

He lifts his head at looks at me with tortured eyes. "All these years you never figured it out. He was never my favorite. You were. Why do you think I sent you away? I wanted to protect you. It was you I loved more."

I bark with laughter. "Protect me. You sent me away so you could play happy families with Linnea and Linnus. It was *Oncle* who took me and protected me. He is my protector. Not you."

He looks at me sadly. "What do you think would have happened to you if I had let you remain in the palace?"

I stare at him with narrowed eyes.

"You would have never made it past childhood, I was convinced of it."

"Why didn't you get rid of her then?"

"I was obsessed with her. It was as if I was under a spell. I knew what she was, but I could not let her go. The only thing I could do for you was send you away from her presence."

"Do you want me to thank you for that?"

"You will never understand me because you are not a weak man. You don't know what it is like to be so utterly bewitched by a cruel and vile woman. You think Cassandra is dangerous. You have no idea."

I shake my head. "I don't care why you sent me away. The time for you to declare your love for me is long past. I don't need your love anymore. I have survived all these years without it! I'm looking forward to being the kind of father to my child that you never were to me. Now all I want from you is the promise that you will send them away and give me the power to rule. You're not interested in ruling anyway."

He sighs heavily. "And if I agree, you will see that your brother receives the revenue he deserves and can remain in Avanti?"

"Yes."

"Then I'll do as you demand, but it's a very hard thing you ask me to do, Dante."

"Your loyalty to her makes me sick," I say.

Our conversation is interrupted by a light knock on the door. A moment later my father's butler enters.

"Your Majesty, you wanted to know when the Queen

returns. She has just arrived." he announces in his booming voice.

Something makes me whirl around to face him. "Where did she go?"

"The hospital, Your Highness."

"The hospital?" I shout before my father can speak.

The butler looks startled. "Yes, I believe Her Majesty went to visit Miss Winchester."

I glance at my father to see if he knows what's going on, but he looks as surprised as me.

I run out of my father's study and I get to meet Linnea as she comes into the house."

"Hello Dante," she says in a friendly voice.

I stride up to her, my face so menacing she shrinks back in fear.

"What are you doing?"

I catch her wrist in my hand. "Why did you go to see Rosa?"

"Let go of me this instant. I am your queen."

"You are not my queen. You never were and you never will be. If you don't talk fast I will break your hand."

"How dare you threaten me?"

I squeeze her pampered flesh viciously and she pales. "Let go of me and I'll tell you. I haven't done anything wrong. I've only tried to help."

I throw her wrist away from me, and she rubs the area where I grasped it. I feel no remorse for having caused her pain.

"You should be thanking me. I helped her. I knew that she would not be safe here so I put her on a plane back to England."

"You did what?" I bellow.

"Don't worry. I sent Elsa with her."

For a full second I stare at her in disbelief. At the audacity of this woman. Then something clicks in my head. It is not audacity. Oh my god. No. I turn away from her. I might still be able to make it. I run outside. The driver who brought Linnea is just about to get into his car and drive off. I push him out of the way and get into the car. I drive through the streets of Avanti like a mad man. I speed through red lights and have two near crashes. I drive right past the security guards. Fortunately, I'm driving the royal car so there is no big commotion. I can see the plane taking off as I approach the tarmac.

"Fuck," I yell. I put my foot on the gas and try to chase the plane. If the pilot sees my car he will not take off, but I am too late. The plane becomes airborne. I get of the car and scream with frustration.

Five seconds after the plane is airborne it explodes and becomes a fireball. I stand there slack-jawed. My brain stops working. I just stare at the trail of black smoke as the fireball falls into the woodlands by the airport.

My legs buckle and I fall on the tarmac. My hands scratch the rough surface until they begin to bleed, but I feel no pain.

CHAPTER 40

Dante
https://www.youtube.com/watch?v=RFnD3uwKHag
How do I live

I should have stayed in Avanti. I should have made them all pay, and God help me I will even if it is the last thing I do, but I can't face any of it just yet. I fly back to Italy. How I pilot the plane is a surprise even to me. I arrive outside her apartment and finally something happens inside me. A sliver of ice thaws.

I fish the copy of her key that I made that morning when I brought her biscuits, out of my pocket and put it into the keyhole. My hand is steady as I push the door open.

I look up at those stairs and the memories, oh, God, the memories they crush me. Her running up ahead of me wearing her long skirt. Another time her bottom in tight white jeans. Laughing. Her laugh. I grit my teeth and take a step into the darkness. I close the door and start up the stairs. My movements are almost robotic.

In the near complete silence, I can hear my heart beating, but my chest feels hollow. I enter her apartment and I have to catch my breath for the astounding pain inside me. It flows in my veins, and strangles my neck. I drop to the ground. The sound of my knees hitting the floor is loud, but I feel no pain. No other pain, but the agony of her loss, can reach me.

It was my fault.

I should never have taken her to Avanti. How could I have been blind? So naïve. So fucking stupid? How can I carry on? My baby is gone. Both my babies. I had so many plans. The house I bought with the rose garden. It had a nursery. It was supposed to be a surprise. My big surprise. Ta da.

I stand up, walk to her bedroom, and sit on her bed.

If I close my eyes I can still see her sleeping, the moonlight on her cheek. How I wish I could turn back the clock. If only I had not taken her. If only I had insisted on following her upstairs when she wanted to change her shoes. I pick up her pillow and smell it. Her scent fills my nostrils and a tearing sound comes from my throat. I bury my face in her scent. *Oh, Rosa, Rosa. Why did you go without telling me? All you had to do was call me.*

"Fuck!"

I can't believe it. I just can't believe she is gone. It is not possible. I don't want to believe it. I want to believe it is mistake, or a nightmare, or an elaborate joke. I want her to come bouncing in here and laugh at me for being so stupid.

The pain is so unbearable I want to howl with it.

I put the pillow back carefully in its place and look around the room. Her alarm clock. A glass of water. Her dry biscuits. I remember buying them that morning. I remember sitting down to watch her eat them. I never wanted to watch a woman eat before. She misread and mistrusted me, but that was another time, another place, another me. I would have done anything for her.

Anything.

I know I have to go back to Avanti. I have to look for her body. I have to avenge her. I have to protect my people from Linnea and Linnus.

But not tonight.

I stand up and go down the stairs. I walk into the pizzeria. It is full of people. The noise and clamor is a shock to my system. It is so noisy it hurts my head. There are people singing and clapping. It could be that I'm in shock, but I cannot make out the words they are singing.

It must be a birthday party because there is a cake with candles on it on the table. So, everything in the world is carrying on as if nothing momentous has happened. As if she is not gone. Antonio calls out to me with his hand.

I walk up to him, my movements are jerky, as if my limbs are being remotely controlled by someone inexperienced at it. He says something, but I don't catch it. He repeats himself and I watch his lips carefully.

"How goes it?" he asks.

"She's gone," I say, my voice trailing, slow. The words are like ashes in my mouth.

"Gone?" he repeats, frowning.

I nod, still unable to believe it. Saying it has not made it real.

"Sit down," he invites, his eyes searching my face.

A waiter brings two glasses of grappa. I down mine and feel nothing. Not even the scrape of it at the back of my throat.

"Give me two bottles," I tell the waiter.

"Immediately," he says.

"Please sit down," Antonio says again, looking concerned.

My mind begins to shut him out, unwilling to deal with

anything else other than my terrible pain. I put some money on the table and look around me, baffled at why I am in such a place. The waiter comes back with the two bottles. I grab them from him and stumble out of the restaurant.

It's too late. Too late to do anything.

I half-walk, half-crawl back up the stairs. I don't switch on any lights so it is as dark as a cave. The silence is strangely soothing after all the happy noises down at the pizzeria. I sit on the floor, unscrew the cap of the bottle, and drink straight from it. I remove the bottle from my mouth and it is half-finished, but the unbearable pain is still there. The grappa has had no effect on me. I take a few more gulps. Grappa is shit when it is not cold, but who fucking cares?

I close my eyes and see the plane bursting into a ball of fire. It can't be real. I drink the rest of the grappa and toss the bottle on the floor. She should be here. I see her pretty blue eyes as she laughs. She should be here. It's not fair.

I didn't even get a chance to tell her I loved her.

I feel so damn empty it feels as if I'm hollow. I open the next bottle and swig a third of it down. I haven't eaten since last night and the grappa starts to take effect. Like a fog inside my skull. Everything is becoming fuzzy except my pain.

I take a few more mouthfuls.

I stand up. My legs feel unsteady. I can't remember the last time I was this wasted. I stagger to her fridge, my mind whirling with crazy thoughts. What did she keep in her fridge? I know so little about her. I don't even know the contents of her fridge. Grabbing the handle, I pull it open.

The light blinds me. I squint until my eyes adjust to the light, then I go closer. Milk, orange juice, butter, a bottle of club soda, two oranges, and a bar of chocolate. They are like a jigsaw puzzle. I try to imagine her buying the chocolate.

Tears start burning the backs of my eyes. I blink them away

and wander aimlessly to her bedroom. It's dark, but I can still see my way to the dressing table. There is a hairbrush there. I've seen it before. I switch on the light.

There is a man in the mirror. His eyes are glossy, too glossy, and his mouth is slack. He looks guilty. I look away from him. I pick up the hairbrush and bring it close to my face. In amongst the bristles I see strands of her flaming hair.

A chasm of grief opens up then.

I remember her saying, "I'll haunt you until eternity."

I begin to cry. I howl like an animal in an abattoir that has smelt the blood and suffering of all the animals who have gone on before it. I will never again be what I was. Sorrow will be my cloak for eternity. The fog of alcohol becomes thick clouds in my brain.

"Dear God, take care of my babies," I whisper as I fall into blackness.

❄

I dream that she visits me. She comes wearing a white dress with red buttons. In my dream I'm so happy to see her. I've been given a second chance. I tell her how much I love her, and she cries. It is so real I feel her tears fall on my cheek. I know it is a dream, but it doesn't matter because I just won't wake up. I never want to wake up.

I tell her I will hold her so tightly I will bring her back into the real world.

In my dream she laughs.

And it gives me goose bumps. That laugh. I'm too gone to get hard, but it is as sexy as fuck. I hold her so tight, determined not to wake up, but try as I can, I can't control my dream. I fall asleep inside my dream.

"Don't go," I whisper as I fade away.

"I'll never leave you," she whispers.

I begin to cry, because it sounds like a lie. I try to hold on, but my fingers start slipping. I can't hold on. "I'm sorry, I can't hold on," I whisper.

"Don't worry. I'll hold you. I'll always hold you because you are my man."

Then it becomes black in my world again.

CHAPTER 41

Dante
https://www.youtube.com/watch?v=cCn4gTCalMI
It's All Coming Back To Me Now

I open my eyes. Sunlight is filtering in through little cracks in the shutters. At first my alcohol marinated brain is too fried to make sense of the patterns on the wall. Where the fuck am I? My head is banging. Fuck, it feels like there is an electric drill in my head. Wincing, I close my eyes. In seconds my eyes snap open. Pain slams back into my body. It is not a gradual affair, but the full wallop in one shattering hit.

She's gone.

I couldn't hold her.

She's gone.

She's never coming back.

Hell, I need more alcohol. There must be more in that second bottle. I pull myself upright.

"Baby."

I freeze. Slowly, very slowly, I turn my head and look at the other side of the bed. My eyes bulge. Rosa! What the fuck? I open my mouth, but no words come out.

"I love you, Dante," she says.

My hand reaches out, trembling, disbelieving, ecstatic, hopeful. I expect my hand to touch air, but it connects with warm flesh.

I twist around and haul her into my arms. I don't care why, or how, or what. I hold her tight. She is mine and I'm never letting her go again.

She makes a small whimper of distress and the sound reaches my brain. I loosen my hold. The bruises. My hands fly away from her.

I look down on her face. "Rosa?"

"It's me, Dante."

"Oh God. This better be real."

"It's real, baby."

"How the hell?" I'm so shocked I can't even get a proper sentence out.

"I didn't get on the plane. I was going to. I was already halfway up the steps when Star's car came onto the tarmac. Remember, I told you she was in Switzerland. She couldn't reach me on my mobile so she called the palace. They told her I had been taken to hospital. So she went there. When she found out I had gone to the airport she rushed there. She made me go with her. I was so frightened for our baby I couldn't think straight or even for myself. I mean, I actually let Linnea convince me it was a good idea to trust her with my life. So I went with Star, but I sent Elsa with my things." Tears start to roll down her face.

"Elsa went down with the plane."

She nods. "Poor innocent Elsa died because I didn't take her with me. I feel so terrible. How could I possibly have known the plane would combust? It never even crossed my mind. I just wanted to talk to Star alone. I was lost. You don't blame me, do you?"

"God, no. I don't blame you, Rosa. Not at all. I love you with all my heart."

She touches my face. "You love me?"

"I love you so much I wanted to die with you."

"Don't say that. Even hearing that hurts me. I'm already so broken with pain. I've been so blind and so stupid. I didn't understand anything. I forgot to trust my own instincts. I trusted all the wrong people. They won't get away with it, will they, Dante?"

"No, you didn't. And no they won't, but it was my fault. I shouldn't have taken you to that vipers' nest."

"I am glad you took me. I have unforgettable memories. It is there I realized I was in love with you."

I smile even though it hurts my head to do so. "It took you that long?"

She smiles back. "When did you find out?"

"I knew you were special straight away, but I didn't want to believe it. Then when you came to Rome to tell me you were pregnant, I knew it was a sign. You were the woman for me."

"Yeah, but when did you find out you were in love with me?" she asks, a cheeky smile on her face.

"You want to know the truth?"

"Of course."

"While I was eating you out that first night in Rome."

"What?"

"I realized you were everything I wanted. Everything about you was perfect. Your smell, your taste, your smile, those sounds you were making while I was sucking your little pussy."

"Really?"

"Yes, really."

"What are you going to do now, Dante?"

"I'm going back. I'm going to fight them," I tell her fiercely.

"How are you going to do that? They seem to be prepared to do anything to keep their power. Even murder."

"I will return and force my father to abdicate immediately. He is sitting on the throne, but it is Linnea and Linnus who are running the show. I told my father I was prepared to keep them in Avanti with a generous allowance, but that was before they tried to blow you up in the plane. I will cut this snake off at the head. I intend to imprison Linnea for treason whether my father likes it or not. He is welcome to remain in the palace and tend to his garden. His life need not change, but I will rule Avanti. It is my duty to my people that their rights are safe-guarded."

"I'll be next to you no matter what," she says softly.

"I'm a better man for having met you, Rosa."

She smiles.

"You don't know what a mess I was yesterday. You just can't even begin to imagine."

She bites her bottom lip. "I'm really sorry, you thought I was dead. It must have been awful for you. I can't even begin to imagine what I would have felt if I had thought you were dead. I tried desperately to contact you, but you switched off your phone. Then we saw the news of the crash on TV, and I knew it was not an accident, but I couldn't get through to anyone. Of course, I knew not to speak to your family.

Finally, I got to speak to Matilda and she told me what had happened. I tried to think what you might have done. So Star got me here in one of her husband's private planes. I went to your hotel, but you had not been there so I came here. I wasn't sure, but I hoped and prayed you would be here."

"It was horrible without you, Rosa. Indescribable. The pain. I thought I was dying. I didn't know how to carry on."

"I'm here now."

"My head is banging, but the only thing I want to do is just fuck you."

"Nope. You are going to take some headache tablets and go back to sleep. When you get up I'll blow you, okay?"

"I'm almost afraid to sleep."

"I promise you we'll be here when you wake up."

"Will you please marry me quickly, Rosa? I love you so much I don't ever want to be without you."

Tears appear in her beautiful eyes. "I love you, baby. I can't even tell you how much. And yes, a thousand times, yes. I'll marry you. As soon as you wish."

EPILOGUE

Rosa

https://www.youtube.com/watch?v=BT4GIljqr-A
(Can't take my eyes off you)

*E*ven though Dante said that he wanted to get married straight away, a royal wedding is an elaborate and grand thing that requires major planning. We have to hire not one wedding planner, but a whole team, and it takes an entire year to plan it. Also, I wanted to lose some weight after the baby was born before I squeezed into my dream wedding dress. The general consensus was I should wear a merengue dress, but I told them where to stick that idea. I always wanted to be a mermaid and this was my opportunity. I went all out, fish tail and all.

So … one year and three months later our wedding date dawns bright and beautiful.

It is the grandest occasion you can ever imagine. I won't be surprised if they find out that the majority of the population attended. What Dante never told me is just how loved he is. The people had been rooting for him and patiently waiting for the day he would take over and be their King.

They come out cheering and waving flags.

Funny thing is after all that time of planning, it passes in a quick blur. Only a few things stand out in my mind. Star, Cindy, Raven and I drinking champagne and laughing while our hair and make-up is being done. Then, when I walk into church and, though Dante had been told during the dress rehearsal not to turn too early, he turns instantly. A slow smile spreads on his face and he shakes his head as if he simply cannot believe his eyes. I try not to trip.

I am so happy.

I remember the brush of his lips after we exchange rings. I remember Matilda putting my son, Alfred Wilhem De-Beau-vouli, into my arms for the photographs. He stole the show. Best looking kid in the world. What can you expect when your father is Dante?

I recall the cake too. White chocolate with raspberry filling, but only because I smear it onto Dante's face. He is a good sport though. He makes me lick it off. The guests go quiet. They don't expect that of their King. Ha, ha, they're going to go quiet a lot in the future. Dante plans to change a lot of things in Avanti.

I remember his Dad. He kisses me on my cheeks and tells me I am the best thing that happened to him, his son, and Avanti. Yeah, I call him Dad. I guess I feel sorry for him. He makes a sad figure. Sometimes I think he still misses for and bleeds for Linnea, though he tries his best not to show it. I guess he truly loved that bitch. We have become great friends. We garden together. The truth is, he should never have been king. He always was, and always will be a gardener at heart.

Unlike him, I never want to see Linnea again. Sometimes I wake up in the middle of the night with strange dreams about her. She caught me at a time when I was so vulnerable she could manipulate me like I was some brainless puppet. Those are the times I think of little Elsa. How she sacrificed that girl as if she was nothing. I still feel guilty about her death. If not for me she would still be alive, but Dante is more pragmatic. He takes good care of her family and tells me what happened is just fate. Some people are born to be princes surrounded by wealth and luxury and other people are born to starve in barren landscapes. She was meant to die on that plane and there is not a thing I could have done to prevent it.

Maybe the person who hurt me the most in all of this was Cassandra. I thought she was a friend. Someone I could have become really close to eventually. How wrong I was. She sent me a card from Dubai, where she and Linnus found refuge. I guess they party there with all the other corrupt despots who have had to flee their countries. The card said: wish you were here. It was a photograph of weathered camel bones in a desert. I don't dwell on any of them for long, or let them keep me awake. I simply roll over and hug Dante, and everything is perfect again.

Oh, of course, I remember the kiss on the balcony. The crowd roars for one more kiss. I blush with embarrassment, but Dante plays up to the crowd, miming that another might overwhelm him. When they good-naturedly beg him for one more, he obliges with a laugh. He sweeps me into his arms and bending me back theatrically, kisses me passionately. Needlessly to say, the crowd eat it all up. I hear cameras clicking like mad. Princess Rosa. Who would have thought? Better than a kick in the teeth, that's for sure.

Then he says, 'Princess Rosa Beauvouli they're playing our song."

And I say, "That's not our song."

And he says, "That was the song they were playing the time I saw you."

And I nearly cry, because I can't believe how lucky I am.

For our honeymoon we fly to Paris. To the Plaza Athenee.

"You know you are the most beautiful woman on earth," he whispers in my ear. I can smell the city in the breeze that blows in through the window.

"You know you are the most handsome man on earth," I whisper back.

"Yeah," he says.

I slap his chest. "Stop being so cocky."

"Why shouldn't I say it? It's the fucking truth. Are you going to deny that wasn't the reason we hooked up in the first place?"

I roll my eyes. "I was very drunk."

"Bullshit. You wanted me so bad I could smell your arousal."

"Haven't you heard of a thing called modesty?"

"Yeah."

"Ever feel like practicing some?"

"Never."

I laugh. "What do you think Alfred is doing?"

"I think he's irritating the hell out of Star."

"Shall we call and find out?"

He takes his phone out, dials and hands it to me. I take it from him. This is the first time I've been away from Alfred and it feels strange.

"Hey," I say.

"I don't think I can give your son back to you," Star says.

I giggle. "He's gorgeous, isn't he?"

"He's so cute, he makes my ovaries hurt."

"What's he doing?"

"It's cute. He's sticking his fingers into the electricity sockets."

I sit bolt upright. "What?"

"Just kidding. He's licking the dog."

"Star!"

"Okay. He's sitting in his cot looking very cross, because I'm talking to you, and not allowing him to crawl around and destroy everything in sight."

"Thank you for taking care of him, Star."

"No probs. Now you better go suck your husband off or something equally carnal and lustful."

"Right," I say. I disconnect the call and turn to my husband.

"Why are you looking at me like that?" he says with a cocky grin.

"Just something Star said."

"What did she say?"

"She said I should suck your dick."

His eyes glow with pure wickedness. "Sounds like very fucking good advice to me," the King says, dropping his pants and showing me his big royal rod.

ONE YEAR LATER

I sit at the vanity brushing my hair. A few minutes later I hear him begin to stir. I turn just as he's getting out of bed.

"Good morning, *bella*," he says, his eyes lingering on my breasts. I know what that means. Horny devil.

"Good morning." I pause. "I want to ask you something."

"Ask away."

"Do you think there are any three-day old biscuits anywhere in Avanti?"

At first he looks puzzled, which makes him look absolutely adorable. I almost jump him. Then, his face breaks out in a disbelieving smile. "You sure?" he asks.

"I'm absolutely certain."

He leaps up, rushes over to me and lifts me clean off the ground.

Our kiss lasts an eternity.

P.S.

I know I did a crappy job of describing my wedding day. If you want more details come over to Avanti, and I'll show you the video over tea and fruit cake. I must warn you though, I look a bit like the cat that got the cream, but Dante and Alfred look amazing.

THE END

COMING SOON...

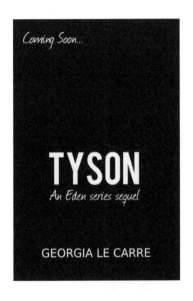

Coming Soon...

TYSON
An Eden series sequel

GEORGIA LE CARRE

EXTRACT FROM TYSON

TYSON

"*A* redhead pulled me aside and asked me a thousand questions about you. Beauty she was too...fucking legs that went up to her neck," Chaz slurs with a sly wink. He's been drinking all afternoon.

I take a sip of my whiskey. "Really, now? Why didn't she come up me herself?"

"I guess she was too shy." He shrugs. "I'm not as intimidating as you. Women see a short guy with a dad bod and automatically think he's easy to talk to. One of the many misconceptions I have to deal with on a daily basis."

I laugh. "Like they don't warm up real quick when they find out how full your bank accounts are."

"If I can keep they hanging around long enough to find out," he points out, laughing.

I scan the room, my eyes traveling over the many firm, half-naked bodies, some of which sway in time with the music pumping out of Brads exceptional sound system. "Which one is she?" I ask, trying to find a redhead among the blondes and brunettes. More than a few of them notice me sizing them up and flash "come hither" smiles my way. I've learned to not let it go to my head…too much. I'm only a man, after all, and with that comes an ego.

"There she is." Chaz points across the room to a small table with four girls sitting around it. Sure enough, one of them is a stunning redhead. Porcelain skin, sapphire eyes, and a body that would tempt the devil himself. Yes, she's very tasty, but it's not her my eyes can't get enough of. It's the girl sitting next to her.

"Who's the girl on her left?" I ask, eyes glued.

"Which one? The blonde?"

"Yeah. The blonde."

"No idea, mate. She's good enough to eat though…"

He's still talking, but I stop hearing him. I can't break focus. The blonde is all I can look at, all I can think about. Her hair shines like gold, and she swings it from side to side as she laughs at something one of her friends said. The light shines directly on her and her eyes are emeralds, sparkling and clear. Her full lips are curves into a smile as she playfully shoves the redhead.

Then, she turns her head and looks at me. She might as well have punched me in the gut. All the air leaves my lungs. Our eyes lock. Fuck me!

"Earth to Tyson," Chaz laughs. "Wow. She did something to you, pal. Do you need a ride to the jewelers to pick up a ring?"

"Stuff it." He's still laughing as I head straight for the table. No way I'm letting her out of my sights. I need to know her. I need to do more than know her.

The girls stop laughing when I approach. One of them

blushes while another looks away. Yes, they were talking about me. The redhead wanted me pushes her chest out.

"Good evening, ladies," I say with a grin. "Enjoying the party?"

They all seem to be at a loss for words. I focus on the blonde. Her wide eyes are trained on me as mine are on hers. The dress she's wearing comes down to her knee, and any man knows that's even sexier than a woman who puts everything on display

"It's nice. Are you enjoying it?" she asks. Her voice drips like warm honey. Hell, I could listen to her read a dictionary.

I lean in. "I wasn't…until just now."

The girls titter with laughter. I don't take my eyes off the blonde. She's really something.

"You're the man of the hour, aren't you? Seems a shame you weren't enjoying a party held in your honor."

"You seem to know a lot about me. I feel at a disadvantage." The way she crosses her long, smooth legs tells me she's interested. She looks me up and down with one eyebrow arched. It makes my cock swell. That look pretty much always guarantees a good night.

She shrugs gracefully. "Why would you know about me? Unlike you, I'm not the most famous horse breeder in England. And I don't make it a point to get my picture in all the juiciest gossip rags, either."

A slow smile spreads over my face. "Yeah, well, I don't make it a point. It just turns out that way. I guess they think I'm photogenic."

She bites her bottom lip. "I guess they do."

It might as well be just the two of us at the table—hell, in the entire suite. The other girls clear their throats a little too loudly before getting up. Funny how on any other night, at any other party, I would've considered any of them a major score. Especially the redhead with the legs that go up to her neck. I barely look at them as I slide into a chair next to the blonde. She smells almost as good as she looks.

"I could keep playing word games with you, but it's all a waste of time." I hold out my hand. "My name is Tyson Eden. But you already knew that, right?"

She nods, placing her hand in mine. It's small, delicate, but her grip is firm. "Izzy."

"Izzy. Short for Isabelle?" Fitting name for a girl like her.

She nods as her cheeks flush. I don't think it's just the wine doing that, just like my whiskey isn't causing my cock to throb—and all from holding a girl's hand. Yup I'm still holding on long after any ordinary handshake would have come to an end. Problem is I want to touch more than just her hand. I want to slide my hand up her skirt and I want to hear her scream when I suck her clit into my mouth.

Hell, if I don't end up between her creamy legs tonight, my name is not Tyson Eden.

****

Tyson Eden's story will be available on pre-order from 23rd September 2017. You'll be able to find the live links on my Facebook page.

AFTERWORD

Thank you for reading everybody!
To receive news of my latest releases please click on the link below.
http://bit.ly/10e9WdE
and remember
I **LOVE** hearing from readers so by all means come and say hello:

https://www.facebook.com/georgia.lecarre

CPSIA information can be obtained
at www.ICGtesting.com
Printed in the USA
FSHW012120170219
55743FS

9 781910 575659